Panic Eyes

Camilla Shelley

WWW.TEHOMCENTER.ORG

Panic Eyes
ISBN: 978-1-960326-66-9
Copyright © 2024 by Camilla Shelley

Tehom Center Publishing is a 501c3 non-profit imprint of Parson's Porch Books. Tehom Center Publishing celebrates feminist and queer authors, with a commitment that at least half our authors are people of color. Its face and voice is Rev. Dr. Angela Yarber.

Panic Eyes

Dedication

To Paul,
for loving all of me,
all the time.

Introduction

I have lived my whole life as a lonely girl in a crowded room. Every decision, every move, every thought has been subject to the captive audience in my own head. I grew up hearing voices cheering me on and tearing me down, too afraid of the consequences to tell any adult what was happening. I was forgetful, losing days and people's names. My friends and family regularly commented on my mood changes and shifts in personality.

I found excuses for all the oddities in my life. If I didn't remember having a certain pair of shoes, it must be because someone else had bought them for me. When I couldn't recall the woman who was hugging me and calling me by name, it was because she must look similar to another lady I knew. It's easy to forget entire days when nothing extraordinary happens. As for the chorus of voices, nobody needed to know about them. If I could keep my sexuality and identity a secret in the deeply religious, conservative south, I could easily keep them a secret, too.

So I lived my life, lonely but never alone. Even after I was married, I held my cards close to my chest. I embraced alcohol with wide open arms and purposely isolated myself from those I cared about. My self worth was at rock bottom, and I lashed out at other women. It wasn't until a sobbing, drunken nightmare brought out all my fears that I admitted to myself that I needed help.

Through therapy, I finally got the words to explain my situation: dissociative identity disorder. I wasn't alone. I wasn't weird. There were other people who could relate. I began to peel back the layers of trauma I endured and how they informed my actions and beliefs. I formally met many of the people inside, and began to understand my role in everything.

I wrote this book in conjunction with therapy, intending to explore a rough time in my life, leading up to that pivotal argument where everything changed. I have always enjoyed writing, and as I poured out the words onto the page, I realized this was what I had been missing. Had I read something that resonated with me and reflected my own life. If I had shared that with those who cared about me, how much would my life have changed? Would I have had the answers sooner? Would I have not felt so alone?

With that in mind, I offer you my story through the lens of Samantha. Her insecurities are my own. Her experiences are my own. I love her as I love myself. I hope her story helps others and gives a glimpse into a life affected by trauma.

CHAPTER ONE

I could feel my skin burning the moment the teacher led us outside. The sun angrily beat down on the class like the wrath of an angry parent, daring us to touch any slide or swing we may encounter that afternoon. I squinted and held a small hand up over my eyes. In the distance, a large splintery jungle gym loomed, its highest tower a small cylindrical blot in the sky.

It was poised over an expanse of sand. There were no dandelions, no honeysuckle, none of the usual hardy plants that came with such a place. Instead, rolling dunes of sand licked desperately at the harsh landscape. Perhaps even more upsetting than the vast desert that stretched before me was the absence of trees. Every playground I had ever been to had trees.

"Strange," I thought, "they should be there."

The ground beneath my feet shuddered a little and a sudden, anomalous gust of wind soared by. I shook the hesitation from my mind and continued with my classmates up to the chain link fence that encircled the playground. We were very orderly, in rows of five, all dressed in matching blue shorts and white shirts. Nobody spoke or looked at each other. We had a mission to carry out- recess.

As we approached, the gate creaked open, hungry for us to fill the sandy void. I watched as kids broke rank and streamed around me, filling the fenced space with a cacophony of laughter and screeches. The teacher stood by, staring blankly at the chaos through her cat eyed glasses. Her black dress billowed around her, pinned in place only by her arms, which were held stiffly at her sides. It was her job to monitor our play, but it gave one the feeling of being a fish in a tank. I smiled and waved at her, but she didn't even blink in return.

"Samantha!"

I turned to see my friends, Rachel and Jen, standing across the field with a bright red kickball. They yelled my name again and tossed the kickball up in the air. Jen caught it and motioned me over.

I began to run towards them. The sand eagerly pulled at my feet, slowing me down. I pumped my legs faster and watched as the ball seemed to move further and further away. Knowing if I stopped, I would be sucked down, I bent my head forward, sweat falling from my brow, and focused on taking big, leaping strides. The sand swirled around my legs, desperate to take me in. I struggled, making large birdlike swings with my arms. Eventually, I made it to the top of the sand where I began to coast along, barely touching it with my foot before kicking off again.

After a few figure eights and a series of skips and hops, I carefully landed next to Jen and Rachel. They were already kicking the ball between them. I eagerly took my place as the third point of a triangle and opened my arms up wide.

"My turn! Kick it to me!"

They didn't respond. The ball continued to roll from Rachel to Jen, Jen to Rachel, slowly, sluggishly. I watched for a few turns, then tried again.

"Guys! Give me a turn!"

Back and forth. Not even a break in rhythm. Neither girl even seemed to acknowledge me. I went up to Rachel and shoved her on the shoulder.

"I said let me in!" I whined. She shuffled to the side and kicked the ball to Jen.

I moved on to Jen, tugging at her arm. "Let me play!" I pleaded. She shrugged me off and made her next kick to Rachel.

I stepped in between them and tried to catch the ball as it was rolling. It swooped around me in a perfect curve before heading straight for Jen.

I was growing frustrated. I blinked tears out of my eyes and yelled, "STOP!"

And just like that, everything did. The screams of the playground, the birds flying overhead, it all stopped. Even the ball came to a halt, resting perfectly between the two girls. I could see the little hashmarks on it; I could almost smell the rubber. I wanted it. I wanted to take it and not let them play anymore.

Suddenly, a hand grabbed my arm with the strength of a metal vise. I looked up to find Rachel, her long brown hair and wispy bangs tangled and falling into her face, framing a slashing, toothy grin.

I didn't have to look. I knew what to expect. As always, though, I found myself rooted to the spot as her head tilted up. Her eyes were a wide, swirling red and black mess. My stomach dropped. Not the panic eyes. This wasn't supposed to happen. This was supposed to be a good day.

Her mouth unhinged and hung agape. In a mirthful tone, she had but one word to say to me.

"Run."

I did. All the kids had stopped to stare, and all had the same eyes. Each one was grinning and laughing; some were pointing at me. The sand tried swallowing me again, but I had learned its trick earlier. I leaned my head down, took giant leaps, and swept my arms in great arcs beside me. When the other children saw me skipping over this deadly trap, they began to lurch towards me.

I screamed for my teacher and ran until I reached her. I looked up at her kind, older face. Blood bubbled from a corner of her mouth, and her eyes were black, swirling with streaks of red. As she slowly grinned, the blood drooled down her chin. She lifted her arms and held them out to me. She opened her mouth to speak, but it was all gibberish. I gasped as I saw why; her tongue had been chewed up. Her smile got wider, and her mouth hung open further. It was as though she enjoyed my shock.

I had to leave immediately.

I ran past the chain-link fence just as it was engulfed by the sand and took my first stumbling steps onto the asphalt. The parking lot that stretched between the school and the playground appeared to go for miles, with nothing on the horizon but more asphalt and the setting sun. I tried running faster, but I was already out of breath. I would have to stop eventually.

I got down on all fours and tried to sprint in that manner. I felt like a mouse on a wheel, running but making no progress. Eventually, a small blip appeared in the distance- the school! As the school came into view, growing closer and closer, I started to leap, pushing up with my arms as well as my feet. Just as I was about to make it, the ground began to shake. A large pit opened up in front of me. I skittered to the edge, peering over into the abyss below. It was completely dark and had no apparent end.

I stood there, feeling a much larger, angrier, singular entity coming closer; every hair on the back of my neck at attention. This was it. This is how it would end. I looked behind me and saw the crowd of children coming towards me. I could feel their eyes on me, could hear their screeching laughter and mocking sounds. They would reach me soon, by the looks of it, and then what? Would the pit be a preferable end? Or perhaps I should surrender to the entity, once it caught up to me?

"Samantha."

I turned around.

A friendly face beamed up at me. She had a head full of dark ringlets and coppery brown eyes. I didn't know her name, but I recognized her instantly, as though she were a part of me. I didn't have to know who she was to know her. Moreover, I was ecstatic that she didn't have the panic eyes.

"Who are you?" I asked, awestruck. She was very pretty, and it made me nervous. She batted my question away.

"Listen to me. There is a way out of this."

"But the pit. It's way too deep", I said, pointing at the chasm.

"No, silly girl," she said, shaking her head. "This is all a dream. You have to wake up."

A dream? The earth began to quake. No. She was wrong, she had to be. This was real, and I was really in danger. I could feel the monster coming closer; the sense of madness clawed at my stomach. The ground started to shake even more violently. A wind picked up and began tearing bits of the school off and sending them into the pit.

Before I could scream, she took my hands. "Close your eyes real tight like this," she said, scrunching her face up, "then open them in the real world! Do it!"

I was panicking, but her voice was steady and calm. It was worth a shot, anyway. I nodded and closed my eyes tight. I strained and gnashed my teeth, focusing hard on escape, but when my eyes opened, it was to her face. She was still smiling, but there was tension there. She knew all too well that we were running out of time. I could hear the children behind me screeching and giggling.

"Again! Do it again!"

I could feel a shift in the air. The monster had almost caught up. I screamed and started to cry. It had never gotten this close before. I had always outrun it.

She squeezed my hands and stared at me sternly.

"Samantha. This is our only way out. I need you to wake up."

I nodded and closed my eyes again. I focused my energy on my eyelids, trying to open them without opening them.

"On the count of three. One . . . two . . ."

The creature's breath was on my neck. It had arrived. It had caught me. This was the end. I screamed.

"THREE!"

My eyes flew open.

CHAPTER TWO

Fifteen Years Later

Samantha's eyes fluttered open. She was in bed, limbs tangled in sheets, hair spewing over the pillows. Her tank top was stained with sweat and she was missing a sock. She laid there for a moment, taking in her surroundings. Four walls, a dingy ecru that she hated, popcorn ceiling she hated even more, and a small window with the screen peeling off. From outside, birds were calling to one another as cars hummed by.

She remembered very little of the nightmare she had just left. It had something to do with a shadowy hallway, disembodied howls echoing off of the broken tile floor. She had been running but not very well. Her legs had felt heavy and slow as if stuck in glue. She tried to recall who or what she had been running from, but her mind produced a hazy blank.

There were no dark corridors or ghoulish screams here, though. The stark contrast took awhile to settle in. She was prone to nightmares, but never quite got used to them, not that anybody really could, she supposed.

Slowly, she sat up, careful not to wake the man sleeping next to her. She plucked her legs from their cotton confines and eased her body up off the bed. The moment she did, she heard a rustling sound. She held stark still and stared at her fiance intently. Eyes closed, he lazily grabbed for the sheets she had just escaped. He brought them close and snuggled in, letting out a deep sigh. So did Samantha, and she crept out of the room.

The wooden floor was cold, but it was better than carpet, she reminded herself. She hated carpet. It seemed there wasn't too much in the world that she didn't hate. Samantha made a mental note to try to be more positive. It was the same note she gave herself every morning, and it had yet to stick.

To my credit, Samantha thought, it's hard to stay positive when you barely sleep.

She flipped the switch in the bathroom, and the light slowly buzzed on. She stuck her face up close to the mirror. Her eyes shone a bright blue despite the thin red lines shot through them. She tugged at the bags under them. No matter what cream or makeup she used, she could never get rid of the blotchy purple circles. She moved on to her chin, where a pimple was starting to emerge.

"Don't do it . . ." came a voice from within.

She ignored it and dug her fingernails into the skin. It popped, and a spot of blood trickled down. She dabbed her face with some toilet paper and looked back at the mirror. There now was a giant, swollen red bump on her face. It looked worse than the zit had.

"I told you," stated the voice cheekily.

"Shut up," she muttered. "Not in the mood."

She dabbed at the spot, but it wasn't getting any better. She sighed and moved on to her hair. It sprung forth from her head in a jumble of curls and waves, its mousy color mocking her. She knew no matter what she did with it, it wouldn't look good. She picked up her brush and dragged it through the mess. This, of course, made it worse, frizzing it into an unkempt halo. Setting the brush down, she grabbed a scrunchie and resigned herself to the usual: messy bun.

She didn't have work that day, but she did have to prepare for the trip they were taking. She considered her makeup and decided it wasn't worth it; she probably wouldn't even get dressed, if she was being fully honest with herself. She tugged at her shorts and examined her tank top. They were perfectly suitable packing attire. She just needed to find that other sock.

She untwisted her shorts from around her waist and pulled them down so she could use the toilet. As she sat, she ran her hands over her legs. They weren't perfectly shaven, but she could probably get by for a few more days.

"One less thing to do," the voice from earlier remarked.

"True," she replied.

"Good thing, too, because you're going to have a lot on your plate this week."

She groaned. "I don't really want to think about it."

"Just keeping you prepared," the voice stated chipperly.

Samantha had been having conversations like these for as long as she could remember. Sometimes, they were pleasant, funny observations. Other times, they were almost parental, like today. The worst days were when they were mean and said awful things about her. Those days she would often call in sick from work and lock herself away in her bedroom.

She finished up her morning routine and crept back into bed. Rob was asleep, still clutching the sheets to his chest. Samantha slipped her arms up against his, carefully prying them apart. He stirred and opened his eyes, staring at her blearily. A moment later, recognition swept his face and he grabbed her up, pulling her in so close she could barely breathe.

"Mmmm, morning sexy," he growled in her ear.

Samantha rolled her eyes, smiling. "Morning yourself."

"Ten more minutes?" he asked. He nipped at her neck.

She wrapped her arms around him. "Ten more, but then we have to get going."

"Yay!" Rob replied, and with that, started to snore lightly.

Samantha stared at him incredulously. "Were you asleep that whole time?"

He snored in reply.

She snuggled down against him. Men, she thought.

"We're not a bad lot" another voice replied.

Never said you were, she thought back.

This was the funny one who would visit sometimes. She was happy to know it wouldn't just be the serious tone all day. Granted, the serious voice would be helpful in keeping her focused and on task, but she needed some levity, too. She could already tell that this was going to be a long, anxiety-inducing trip.

Her fiance was deeply into online gaming and streaming. They were going to a convention to meet some friends in real life and get a peek at some of the latest projects in the industry. Samantha planned to hit up the merch booths and do some shopping for most of the convention, maybe playing some new releases. She knew Rob was going to be the man everyone flocked to, mister social butterfly in the flesh, and the thought of being swept up in that gave her a near panic attack. No, it would be shopping, some gaming, and a lot of time in the hotel watching movies.

It wasn't that Samantha hated people. She found them fascinating, enjoyed their company one on one, but large crowds always caused her grief. The thought of so many people staring at her, judging her, questioning her existence terrified her. She would start to hyperventilate, her legs would tense up, and her hands would shake. Having Rob next to her helped; he grounded her in a way nothing else could. She hoped this would be enough to get her through their trip. She was looking forward to it, but the anxiety was beginning to creep in.

When it became clear that ten minutes was not going to be enough for Rob, she wrestled herself away and grabbed her missing sock from the foot of the bed. Her stomach grumbled as she bent over to slip the sock on. She knew she would need to eat something soon, but her nerves would tide her over for now.

She walked over to the closet and pulled their suitcases off of the top shelf. His was a rugged, but smart, green case. Hers, on the other hand, was a large, worn out shell missing a wheel and half of its zippers. She found them to be very fitting representations of themselves.

Rob was a big, rugged kind of guy, with sparkling green eyes that always brought a sense of mischief to his face. He was very intelligent and incredibly kind, an absolute gentleman. Samantha, on the other hand, always had a worried look about her, as if everything were going to go wrong at any moment. She was a little broken, she often said about herself, but it was this brokenness that attested to her strength and willpower. While Rob grew up comfortably, Samantha's parents were poor. She had to help take care of her brothers while her parents worked and would often do the cooking, cleaning, and pet care, as well. She juggled this with school, where she was bullied regularly. Rather than feel shame about it, she preferred to see it as something that had built her up, something she had overcome. Instead of quitting school, she had graduated out of spite and ahead of most of her bullies.

It was in college that she had met Rob. She was an awkward freshman, and he was a popular senior. If it weren't for a run in at the theatre, they may have never crossed paths. He was quick to take her under his wing and helped socialize her, encouraging her to join clubs and attend events. During performances, he would sneak into the dressing room and leave uplifting notes for her to find. In her senior year, he would take her away from campus to rest and destress. He was always there for her.

She ran her hand over her bag. It still served its purpose, still carried on, and so would she. Samantha gave it a little smile before pulling both next to the bed where Rob still slept. She considered hoisting them up to the empty side and getting started when her stomach yowled at her. With a sigh, she nudged the bags closer to the bed, then headed over to the kitchen.

The kitchen was large and opened up into the living room. Cabinets lined all three walls and a small table sat in the middle. It was rarely a calm, clean sight. Even now, dishes were piled in the sink and on the counter. The table still had last night's dinner sitting on it. Samantha groaned. Rob went to bed later than she did, and she always asked him to put the leftovers away. He rarely did.

"Men, am I right?" the funny voice said.

Haha, Samantha thought. She let out a sigh and began to tidy up. Eventually, enough space was cleared for her to start cooking some oatmeal. She liked it best with blueberries, and pulled a container out of the fridge. To her dismay, they were covered in white and green fuzz.

How long ago did I buy these, she wondered. She threw them away sadly and resigned herself to regular oats with a little brown sugar. While the oatmeal was cooking, she started the kettle for tea. It was the old school silver type, with a fat bottom and a curving black handle. Her friends often teased her and suggested an electric kettle, but she preferred the method, filling it in the sink, setting it over the flames on the stove, hearing it whistle when it was ready. It reminded her of when she was little and helped make tea with her grandmother.

Nearly an hour later, she sat sipping some tea when Rob rounded the corner. His hair stuck up on one side, and he gave her a sleepy smile.

"Any left for me?" he asked, motioning to the empty bowl in front of her.

"Sure, plenty of oatmeal to go around!" she replied with a smirk.

Rob pulled a face. "Nevermind. I'll grab some toast," he said.

"When did you get to bed anyway?" Samantha asked.

Rob cringed. "Aaaaah, you know," he said, "four or five."

"Dude," Samantha said. "What were you even doing?"

"I had a lot of people watching; I couldn't just leave them hanging."

Samantha rolled her eyes, but left it alone. He shot her a quick glance.

"How did you sleep?"

Samantha waved a hand. "I slept fine."

"That's Samantha for 'I had nightmares all night', isn't it?" he asked pointedly.

"It's fine," she reasserted. "I'll be fine. Now, about this trip . . ."

Rob sighed and returned to his toast. Samantha cleared her throat.

"So, we pack today. Then we need to get your cards made, right?"

"I got them made, just need to pick them up."

"Did you get the kind you wanted? I know there were a lot of different styles last year, and you want to stand out."

"I did and with a discount!" Rob replied cheerfully. This wasn't his first convention, but it was his first one as a recognized creator. He needed to make an impact while he was there in order to grow further in the field.

"Perfect!" Samantha exclaimed. "Then we need to get those little travel size supplies."

"What, hotel shampoo not good enough for you?" Rob asked mockingly.

"It takes work and good product to have hair this frizzy," she replied dryly.

Rob slipped his toast onto a plate and sat down across from her. He nudged her feet with his.

"Just teasing. Of course we need to get that stuff. Little deodorants, tiny body wash, the whole miniature bathroom set."

Samantha nodded sagely. "Only the smallest will do."

"Then, we need to get you a dress."

She set her mug down and stared at him quizzically. "I have dresses."

"Right, but let's get you a new one. A fancy one!"

"Rob . . . why?"

He grinned sheepishly at her. "There's an after-party type thing that I'd like you to attend with me."

Samantha's stomach fell. "Oh, okay. Who all's going to be there?"

Rob shrugged. "Some of the guys, a few of their wives and girlfriends. Just a mix, really."

She let out a mental sigh of relief.

"He's lying," a little voice creeped in. "That girl's going to be there. The one that flirts with him, the one he flirts back with. She's going to be there all dressed up and looking perfect, and you're going to roll in there all fat and dumpy, and they're going to be all over each other, and you-"

Samantha took a deep breath. "Sounds like fun. Where's it at?"

"We're going to meet up for dinner, and after that head to Jason and Todd's suite."

She nodded. Jason and Todd were safe. She had met them before and they seemed nice enough. Jason could be a little high strung, but Todd evened him out. They both worked at the same game studio, but when asked, they could never quite describe exactly what it is they did. As best as Samantha could tell, Jason worked with the actual coding of the game, while Todd did design work. They were also clearly hooking up, though neither would admit to it.

"But she's not safe," the voice interrupted. "What are you going to do about her?"

Samantha blinked. What would she do if Cassie were there? If she left, she'd look weak or snobby. If she stayed, it would eat her up inside. She knew logically that Cassie was just another creator, one of thousands that would be there, and that her flirtiness was as much a performance as it was a marketing tool. It was a tactic that, when used successfully, brought in more promotions, more revenue, and more opportunities. The insecurity that Samantha felt, however, was an entirely different story.

"She's a whore" the voice spat.

"And we are cutting that off," the pleasant voice from earlier butted in. "You will look fabulous, and Rob will be focused on you. You're safe."

Thank you, Samantha thought.

"Any time you need it,' the voice replied.

"You still there?" Rob asked.

Samantha jumped a little.

"Hmm? Yes, absolutely," she replied.

"I lost you for a minute," he said, eyeing her inquisitively.

"Just thinking about what kind of dress I want," she offered.

Rob smiled and finished up his toast. "Something sexy", he said.

"Of course. It is me we're talking about," Samantha replied sarcastically.

Rob leaned over and gave her a kiss. "Hahaha, but really. It's been awhile since you've had a cute little red dress to wear. Something like that?"

"Sounds good. You're the one who has to be seen with me."

"And I will love every minute of it," he said, putting his plate in the dishwasher.

I hope so, Samantha thought.

After breakfast, they hoisted the bags onto the bed and began to fill them with clothes. They were going to be gone for nearly a week. It took Samantha longer than Rob, as she second guessed everything she pulled from the closet. That thin voice that had creeped in hadn't said anything else, but the impact it had from earlier still shook her. This skirt was way too short; it would show off all her cellulite. These shorts were too long and made her legs look chunky. This shirt showed off too much cleavage, but this shirt didn't show off enough. She started to feel fuzzy, as if she were half asleep. These shoes were cute, but were the heels too high? Would she look like a slut?

Would she look like Cassie?

This thought caused her to stop altogether, clutching a thin, blue shirt. Her eyes focused on the shirt, and the calming color pulled her in. Voices swirled inside her head, rapidly hurling accusations and observations at her. Even they eventually became a fuzzy, white noise in a sea of blue.

With a start, Samantha blinked, and the shirt was gone. Instead, she found herself playing a video game. Her gear was lower tiered, and she hadn't made it very far into the level she was on, so she couldn't have been playing for long. Unless I was playing something else first, she thought. An eerie feeling began to flow over her, settling into a heaviness in her stomach. She shook it off, saved the game, then wandered through the apartment to the living room where Rob was watching a movie. He looked up at her and paused the film.

"There you are. Ready to get that dress?"

Samantha looked at him suspiciously. "Don't we have to get your cards?"

Rob pointed to the suitcases by the door. "That's what I just ran out to do. When you told me you needed a break. I figured I'd let you get some gaming in while I took care of it. I also picked up our tiny toiletries and some makeup wipes for you."

Samantha swallowed. She had asked for a break? She had been tired all morning, and the thought of the trip was stressful. It made sense she'd need one. Of course she had asked for a break.

"Ah, right," she said. "In that case, let me get put together, and we'll head out."

Once she was ready, they made their way outside to the car.. Rob drove while Samantha watched the city go by out the window. She remembered packing, and she remembered playing video games. Sometimes, if she back tracked enough, she could dredge up some other details, but nothing was coming up. I must have been very tired, she thought. Her gaze moved to the park they were passing. The trees reminded her of her parent's place. They lived far out into the country, with nobody around for miles. Her parents loved the privacy it gave them, but Samantha always felt it was isolating. There was nobody her age to play with, nowhere to go, nothing to do.

"Nowhere to run," a voice quietly added.

At the store, Samantha felt uneasy. The place was filled with beautiful, stylish people and the clothes being sold reflected that.

She didn't belong. The salespeople were very enthusiastic, and it made her feel guilty. Can't you see you have the wrong customer, she wanted to say. Rob was patient with her and slowly went through aisle after aisle with her, waiting outside the dressing room for her to try on the latest find. It took a few hours, but they finally found a cute, off the shoulder red dress. Samantha was worried that it was too tight in the chest, but Rob seemed to love it.

Mission accomplished, they headed home, stopping for burgers along the way.

"To go?" Rob asked.

Samantha nodded. "Please. I've been out enough for one day."

Rob nodded with understanding and pulled up to the drive thru.

On the way home, Samantha continued to fret about how the convention was going to go. If she had trouble getting through the store, how was she going to handle a whole convention center full of people?

Rob says the room has a big tub, she reminded herself, and the Netflix queue is full. Everything will be fine.

"Then why are you going in the first place?" a voice wheedled. "You can watch Netflix in a tub at home."

Samantha was taken aback. Of course she was going; Rob was going, so she was, too. She enjoyed gaming, and that was the convention's focus. Why wouldn't she want to attend?

"Rob is there for a reason," the voice continued. "He's there for his career, his passion. Do you even have a passion? A purpose? Any reason for existing?"

I don't, she sadly admitted to herself. When Rob first started streaming, it was like watching a Christmas tree light up. He immediately fell into it with an infectious exuberance that drew his audience in close. He had a track, goals, dreams, all related to his content. He was always interested in marketing and game promotions, and content creation naturally fell into that realm. This convention was his opportunity to dive into that world and build his platform. It would give him a foot in the door to the world he had wanted to join for so long.

Samantha, on the other hand, worked as a teller for a big bank that valued her sales more than her promise. She took the job after college, where she studied theatre. She had been told by numerous people that it was a dead end path, but she enjoyed it. Many of her classmates had gone on to have successful careers in the field, but Samantha was never able to point herself in a specific direction. She often joked that she was good at many things but never great at one. It was true that she had no reason to attend the convention, other than passing interest, just as it was true that she didn't really have a purpose in life. She drifted aimlessly and in that drifting, felt isolated and meaningless.

She spent the rest of the ride in sad silence. Rob must have sensed her shift in mood, as he reached over with one hand to rub her shoulder while he drove. He didn't say anything, but Samantha preferred that he didn't. This was something for her to wrestle with on her own.

Once they were home, they curled up on the couch with their food. Rob turned on a stream for them to watch while they ate, and Samantha was able to take her mind off of the anxieties that had plagued her that day.

"Do you think a lot of people will recognize me?" Rob asked, staring at the guy on the tv. He was sporting a large, bulky headset and a pair of yellow tinted glasses. The way he yelled at each turn in the game, you would have thought he was an exuberant sports announcer, if not for the giant pink bunny in the background of the video. Rob seemed to be studying him more than watching him.

Samantha thought for a moment. "I think so. You've been letting everyone know you're going to be at the convention, so there will definitely be people expecting you."

She snuggled up to him and stole a fry in route to his mouth. "I'm going to have to fight off the crowd to be with you," she said, popping the fry in her mouth.

Rob frowned and swatted her arm. "Pfft, you're not getting away that easily. You'll be right there next to me for as long as you want."

He pulled her close and whispered in her ear, "And if you want to leave early, I may be inclined to join."

Samantha pulled away and looked at him. Rob winked, green eyes twinkling mischievously. "Oh, really?" she asked.

He nodded solemnly. "Whenever you want."

"Like now?" she asked, raising an eyebrow.

Rob didn't answer. Instead he set his fries down on the table and leaned over to Samantha. He grabbed at her waist, but she stood up before he could. He got up and chased her into the bedroom, slamming the door behind him.

While the convention and missing chunk of time were far from Samantha's thoughts, there were still whispers in the back of her mind taunting her about a woman she had never met.

Chapter Three

The wind was biting. It whisked dry brown leaves along the sidewalk in small torrents. The trees that lined the street danced to and fro, dropping more leaves as they went. Out from behind one of these trees crawled a small white mouse.

I watched, curious, as he scurried over to me. He stood up on his hind legs and pawed at his whiskers, staring through my eyes and into my soul with his own blood red orbs. I slowly knelt and stretched a cupped hand out towards him, inviting him to come closer. He wriggled his ears in defiance and took off running, looking back only once before rounding a corner.

I stood up and took in my surroundings. Beyond the trees were old fashioned storefronts. Brightly colored awnings hung over large windows with boldly painted signs. Some displayed hats, others stationery, and another a collection of small pianos, one of which was being played by a black and white cat. Without needing to see a sign, I knew this was a "Main" street. Cute wooden benches with twirling iron arms sat outside each store, and flower pots were tucked into every corner. The street itself was surprisingly narrow, and the buildings on the other side mirrored their counterparts exactly. There was another store with small pianos and the same black white cat. The awnings were all the same colors, the flowers all the same, even the trees were shaped similarly.

There were no cars in the street, and the sidewalk was deathly quiet. Although it was a beautiful day outside, nobody strolled by, the jingle of bells in shop doors did not ring out, and there were no friendly dogs on leashes to greet me. Why was everything so empty?

It hit me.

This isn't real.

The sidewalk slowly lifted and buckled, folding in on itself like an accordion. The trees and buildings began to lurch around me as though swept up in a tornado, their images dragging and elongating like they were being stretched and pulled apart. I cried out and clawed at a passing branch, hoping to steady myself. The branch flew away just as a large, dark chasm began to open in the street. My legs crumpled underneath me, and I landed square on my bottom. Panicked, I started scrambling backwards, watching the world spill into a whirlpool mere inches from my feet. All the structures melted into an amalgamation of color and fuzzy shapes. The chasm was widening, and I stared in horror as it quickly overtook me, my feet falling over the edge, stretching painfully into void. Just as I felt the pull, a hand fell on my shoulder.

I jumped and turned my head to see a tall, blond man standing behind me. His hair hung in his eyes as he gave me a crooked grin.

"Here, let me help you up."

I turned back to the whirlpool but it was gone; I hadn't even noticed the tugging sensation leave. The street had righted itself, and the trees had resumed their slow dance. Although everything had returned to idyllic Americana, something had to have sparked the mayhem I had just witnessed. I tried mentally retracing my steps. The mouse sauntering away, the trees slowly swaying, the brightly colored awnings hanging over glossy windows, the piano store with the black and white cat, and on the other side of the street-

"Oh, no, none of that," the blond man interrupted, "come on."

He grabbed my arms and hoisted me up. I turned around fully and found that I barely came up to his shoulders. He put his hand back on my shoulder and looked me in the eye. His green eyes sparkled with mischief, but also betrayed some concern.

"You have to be careful how much you notice. If you overthink things, that will happen again."

I was confused. "So, what should I do then?", I asked.

His grin grew wider. "You came here. What do you want to do?"

I shrugged. "It seems like a nice place; should I just relax?"

"Hmmm…" he replied teasingly "Relaxing? Been stressed lately?"

"I guess you could say that," I answered. "I always did enjoy playing on the hardest difficulty."

He laughed, delighted at my little joke. "You need to take life easier, then. Smell the roses." He looked down at one of the flower pots. "Or begonias. Or pansies. I'm not sure what those are. But those, smell those!" He picked a red geranium, what was actually in the pot, and handed it to me. Obligingly, I took a sniff. The strongest floral scent swirled around me in a glittery haze of pink smoke. I could have practically drowned in it. I must have looked shocked because he started to laugh again. "Isn't it nice? Don't get that effect at home."

I popped the flower behind my ear, watching the aura of its scent whisk away with it. "What is this place, exactly?" I asked.

His grin slipped into a more relaxed smile. "It's whatever you need it to be."

"Who lives here, I mean?"

"Anybody who needs to," he replied.
I started to feel frustrated.

"Then who are you? Why do you need to be here?"

32

His smile fell a little. "I don't live here. I came because you needed me."

"But who are you?"

He tilted his head. "You know me, Samantha. I can assure you, you know me quite well."

I couldn't deny that I had that feeling. But the name was escaping me, and I could not remember how I knew him. Was he one of Rob's friends?

He shook his head. "The name's Eric, darling."

The name traveled around in my head a moment. Eric . . . it certainly felt familiar. It settled into the nooks and crannies of my mind, engulfing everything like a warm sweater. Eric, he said. Where had I heard that name?

Suddenly, it hit me.

"You! You're the funny voice!"

His grin was beaming again. "Aw, thank you! I do my best."

"But how? Is this a dr-"

"Ah!" he interrupted sternly. "If you think about it too much, it'll just break down again."

I nodded. "Understood. It's just so weird! I mean, it's great, too!"

I awkwardly stretched my arms out, and he nodded, motioning me to bring it in. I gave him a big hug, and the smell of freshly washed linen poured over me erupting into swirls of light blue that faded slowly into the air.

"How long has it been since I started hearing you? I feel like I've known you forever!"

"In some way, you have," he replied.

I pulled back and held him at arm's length. I looked him over from beat up sneakers, to jeans, to unbuttoned collar, all the way to the top of his head. "It's really you."

He arched an eyebrow and held his arms out in a half shrug. "It really is."

He motioned for us to sit on one of the benches. At this point, the strangeness of my surroundings had left me. It was like being with one of my oldest, closest friends.

"So, really," I asked, once we were settled in. "Why are you here?"

"Like I said, you needed me," he answered. "I reckon this whole convention thing has gotten you all in a tizzy."

I nodded.

"Listen," he said, slinging an arm around me, "I will always be here for you, okay? We will tell that Cassie chick to lay off our man if we need to. I will keep you laughing and happy, and we will get through this together. I am here for you."

"Our man?" I asked teasingly.

His eyes sparkled. "Oh, what, you have a monopoly on Rob? I can't enjoy some Rob time?"

We both laughed. "I like Rob," he said. "He seems like a nice guy, and you two are a perfect match! You have nothing to worry about, understand?"

Out of the corner of my eye, I spotted the mouse at the end of the street. He was still staring at me intently. He slowly raised his paws to his whiskers and began grooming himself, never breaking eye contact. I chose to ignore it for the time being.

"Of course," I said. "You're right. I'm being silly about all of this."

He leaned in close to me and whispered conspiratorially, "Besides, Cassie is raging alcoholic; even she knows she's trash."

I slapped his arm, mildly horrified. "Eric! What is wrong with you?!"

He laughed again. "See how quickly you come to her defense? Why can't you do the same for yourself?"

I paused. Why couldn't I?

"We'll get you a backbone built up, a shiny steel spine," he said. "Soon you'll be too cool and confident for anyone to get to you. We just need to get you out of your head first."

"But that's where you are," I replied.

He paused for a moment and gave me a peculiar, skeptical look. It seemed that I had said something that he didn't find to be completely true.

"It is, isn't it?" I asked. "That's where I hear you, anyway."

As I asked, the mouse caught my attention again. He had put his arms down and was sniffing the air. He abruptly turned his head to look at something around the corner; he stared for a moment, as if watching something. He then sank back down onto all fours and ambled away.

"What do you keep looking at?" Eric asked quickly, changing the subject.

I jumped a little. "Oh, just some mouse that keeps staring at me. He's kinda cute, like one of those little maze mice."

Eric jumped up. "Where? What does it look like? Is it just the one?"

"Yes, a little white mouse," I answered, puzzled, "just down there."

He swallowed and turned to me. His grin had disappeared and his face had gone pale. "You stay there. Let me handle this."

With that, he took off running down the street and rounded the corner where the mouse had been.

"Eric, wait!" I shouted, standing up.

The wind blew through the trees again, kicking the leaves up in the street. I stood a moment, craning my neck to see if Eric was coming back, but I had lost sight of him. I wanted to follow, but at the same time, I felt that I couldn't. After a few minutes of waiting, I turned to peer into the shop windows. The shop with all the miniature pianos caught my eye first.

Each instrument was meticulously crafted. All the keys, all the strings, tiny pedals, everything was the same as a full sized piano. The smallest one could fit in the palm of my hand. I turned my attention to the cat playing the mini grand piano. He wore a small red bow tie, his paws poised over the keys. He seemed real, as though you would catch him breathing any moment. As I had that thought, one paw dipped down and struck a key, the tone seeming to echo throughout the universe.

I felt a wave of panic, but couldn't move.

I stared as the other paw joined in. The cat's head began to nod and sway as his feet worked the pedals. The music rushed over me in much the same way as the flower's aroma had. I felt swept up in it, held in place by it. Languidly, the cat began to turn his head until his eyes met mine. They were black, with ribbons of red swirling in them. His mouth fell open into a grinning maw.

Before I could scream, hands were on my shoulders, pulling at me.

"We have to go," Eric said. "Now."

We began to run down the street in the opposite direction from where the mouse had been. As we ran, the street grew longer, and the stores stretched in front of us like they were made of silly putty. The trees bent, shaking their leaves menacingly above us.

"This isn't working," I shouted. "We have to turn back."

As I twisted around, I could hear Eric begin to yell something, but it was muffled. Everything had fallen into slow motion. When I was fully turned, the sidewalk and stores all zoomed back into position, but someone had appeared.

A little girl was standing at the end of the block, holding the mouse in her hand. She wore a knee length white dress with puffed sleeves and ribbons. She had long, blonde curls and bangs that fell into her eyes. Her eyes were jet black, with red globules swirling in them. She did not smile or approach though. Her demeanor was one of sadness. She held the mouse out towards me. I took a step towards her to accept it, but Eric stopped me.

"Don't," he said. "Just slowly back away and focus on a different place. We don't have to be here. Did you want to go to the beach? I hear the water's great this time of year."

I felt drawn to her, though. I wanted to see who she was, what she and the mouse meant. I took another step forward.

"Samantha, no! They'll be here any moment. We have to go!" he shouted angrily.

As if on cue, people began to round the corner. They all had the panic eyes. Unlike the girl, however, they all had their faces twisted into diabolical grins. Some shrieked, others giggled, they all made some sort of uncomfortable noise. They started to lurch towards me. The little girl held her place, despite being under waist height to most of them. They swarmed around her, reaching for me.

"It's too late!" Eric cried with a frustrated groan. "You have to wake up!

I swallowed and nodded. Before I closed my eyes, I looked for the little girl one last time. She was staring at me, arm still outstretched. The mouse had stood up on its hind legs again. They were both stock still, seemingly unbothered by the chaos surrounding them.

I closed my eyes and began to mutter. "Wake up. Wake up. C'mon."

My eyes opened. The crowd was mere feet away.

I closed my eyes again, scrunching my nose up, focusing as hard as I could. "Wake up. Wake up."

I felt hands grabbing at my arms and face. I screamed, "Wake up!!"

Like magic, my eyes opened to my bedroom. I could hear my fiance asleep next to me. Safe. We were safe.

I tried to roll over to look at him, but found myself frozen. I tried blinking, sitting up, rolling again, all to no avail. Frightened, my heart began pounding in my ears. No matter how many times I woke up in this state, I would never get used to it. I frantically tried wiggling my big toe, then my index finger, anything I could use to pull the rest of me out of this.

"Okay," I thought. "One big heave?"

I braced myself and counted down from five. On one, I flung my left arm over my body. I watched as another, fainter arm lifted from my real one. It created a rainbow of arms behind it, as if it were lit by a strobe light. This seemed like progress, some type of movement at least. I focused on doing the same with my torso. Five count, on one, ROLL.

It worked! I was laying on my side, despite being somewhat outside my body. When I looked back I could just barely see my body still lying face up in the bed. As the implications of the situation began to dawn on me, I spotted movement towards the bedroom door.

The girl I had seen in my nightmare was in my room. She calmly walked around the bed, coming up beside me. She still had panic eyes and a solemn expression. Sitting on her shoulder was the little white mouse. They both stared at me. I tried to talk, but no words came from my throat. The next thing I knew, I had flown back into my body. I tried flinging myself out again, but I was thoroughly frozen.

Out of the corner of my eye, I saw the little girl take the mouse and place him on my bed. I heard him scurry over to me. His tiny hands grasped sections of my hair, tugging them out of his way. I felt his whiskers on my ear, then his paws. To my horror, what followed next was a digging sound. I could not scream, but I could feel him burrowing into my head through my ear. I rolled my eyes over as far as they would go. The girl was standing, watching. Her face betrayed no emotion over what was happening. I mentally pleaded with her to do something. She tilted her head, but stayed still otherwise.

As I listened to the mouse chewing and digging into my brain, I refocused on my index finger. If I could just get it to wiggle, maybe I could wake up. Slowly, my fingertip rose, then my knuckle, then my hand, then my-

Chapter Four

Samantha woke with a start. Her heart was racing. She sat up in bed, soaked in sweat. With one hand, she reached out for Rob. With the other, she checked her ear. Everything was intact; there was no gaping hole as she expected. Rob was fast asleep. If any movements had come through, none had been frantic enough to wake him.

Sleep paralysis was something Samantha dealt with regularly, and it almost always came after a nightmare. She tried retracing her steps mentally. She remembered the mouse and the girl had been in the nightmare as well as the paralysis. There was also something about a cat, though that seemed less important.

Her biggest question was who was the girl with the panic eyes but none of the behavior? She seemed so calm and in control of herself, not typical features of the swirling red ocular event. Moreover, why was there such sadness about her?

Samantha eased her body out of bed and padded her way into the kitchen. She opened the pantry and stared at it blankly for a few moments before pulling out a box of lavender tea. She filled her kettle and turned on the stove. Her actions left her feeling disembodied, as though she were a shell just going through the motions. This wasn't unheard of after a bout of paralysis, and she had been fuzzy earlier in the day. Despite the familiarity, she still hated that hollow sensation. It made her feel like a character in a video game- physically present but being controlled by someone else.

The rotten cherry on top of the shit sundae, she thought.

She sat at the table, slowly pulling in bits of the nightmare. She remembered there was talk about Cassie, though the specifics had left her. Of course she would have been a part of all of this. Samantha groaned. If it weren't bad enough that everyone else was obsessed with her, now Cassie was living rent free in her head, as well. She buried her head in her arms.

"I bet she isn't a weirdo with nightmares," piped up the same thin voice from before.

"With as much as she drinks, I'm sure she is," quipped a laid back voice.

Samantha's head shot up. "Eric!" she exclaimed, memories of the dream flooding back.

There was no answer, though.

She sighed and settled back into her chair. Rob had met Cassie a year or so before. They played similar games, so their audience overlapped some. She was quickly gaining a following and would regularly reward that following with semi-nude pictures. Her stream was never complete without her cherry red hair, low cut tank top, and a push up bra. She bounced for follows, wrote the biggest donors' names on her body, and called her subscribers her "sexy kittens".

It made Samantha insecure on a level she wasn't ready to grapple with. She was always an advocate for building women up, but something about this stopped her in her tracks. Samantha had enjoyed gaming from a young age but was often told that it wasn't for girls. She felt as though nobody had ever taken her seriously because of this. Some of those emotions still lurked there for her when seeing women like Cassie take over the scene, that given their behavior, she would never be taken seriously. If pressed for reasons to dislike them, though, she would falter.

It also didn't help that she was particularly flirty with Rob. Samantha knew they had conversations often. She had seen him minimize the chat when she walked in the room. They often tagged each other in tweets and did co-op streams together. He knew how Samantha felt; they had even had a few arguments about it.

Rob always told her that the two women would be close friends, if Samantha just gave her a chance, but she knew that would never happen.

"She's a gamer!" Rob had said. "Just like you!"

"No, Rob," Samantha interrupted. "I don't play games with my tits out."

"Well, maybe you should," he joked.

It was the wrong joke to make.

Samantha retorted that if that were the case, she may as well just be a camgirl and get paid more than her bank job. Rob then angrily asked if she were calling Cassie a whore, to which she replied, "if the bikini fits", referencing the swimsuit shots Cassie posted previously that Rob had liked and shared. The argument ended with him berating her about her low self-esteem and how she needed to stop policing what other women did simply based on her own self hatred.

Samantha wanted to reply that her self hatred could stem from the folder of pictures she had found on his desktop when ordering pizza one day. The fact that all the women looked very much like Cassie and very little like herself did not make for a very secure self image. She didn't want him to know that she had seen that folder, so she didn't say anything. She had walked away from the argument and cried in her room. She would look down at her body periodically since then and imagine taking a knife and cutting away all the excess and all the flaws. The same argument would come up repeatedly, and each time, she would spiral into a deep depression.

The whistling of the tea kettle brought Samantha back into the present. Her whole being trembled, and she felt as though she had left her body for a moment. She shakily stood up and tiptoed to the stove, quietly turning the burner off. Samantha prepared her tea the way she always liked it, with two spoons of sugar. She returned to her chair and curled up around the mug in her hands.

She had tried to keep up with Cassie for a while after their first fight. She barely touched food, worked out aggressively, wore provocative clothing to keep her fiance interested. It didn't work. He still minimized his chats, still talked with her over games, and would often shoo Samantha away to go to bed alone. It may have been simple jealousy on her part, but it hurt. She decided that if she couldn't keep up, she may as well give up.

Now, she had gained a good amount of weight, her hair was always a mess, and she couldn't remember the last time she liked her makeup. Her self esteem was at an all time low, and she felt a deep, true hatred for herself. She would never measure up to the woman on the other side of the screen.

"Maybe you shouldn't go to the convention," a reassuring voice stated.

"Oh, and leave Rob and Cassie alone to do God knows what," the thin reedy voice replied.

Samantha took a sip of her tea and let the lavender seep into her soul. Did she trust Rob? Of course she did. Did she trust Cassie? Not in a million years.

"You can just stay in the hotel," the reassuring voice said.

"While Rob and Cassie go to that schmoozy party," the reedy voice added. "I bet they'll get a few drinks in them, start cuddling up real close. Maybe she'll even do that little bounce thing for him. She may not even have to write his name on her body; I bet he'll be happy to do it himself."

"Enough!" Samantha said, banging her mug on the table and tearing up. "I'm done. We are going to the convention, we're going to have fun, and nobody is going to ruin it for us. Least of all, her."

She took a few sips of tea and stared blankly across the room.

"Rob will be there, and he will look out for us. It will be fine."

A flurry of thoughts were rising up inside her mind. Her weight, her appearance, all those people, how weird she acted, they would all hate her. The thoughts overwhelmed her. They're all going to hate you, stupid girl, fat girl, unwanted, unloved, no place for you, ugly girl, they're all going to hate you.

She went to banish the thoughts with another sip of tea, only to be surprised to find it cold. A chill swept her body. It had been piping hot moments earlier. It was pretty late; maybe she had fallen asleep for a moment?

Samantha nodded, dumping the rest of the cup down the sink. She was very tired; the tea had definitely done its job.

She made her way back to bed, where Rob was curled up into a ball. She pried his arms apart and settled into them.

He stirred and mumbled, "I love you."

Samantha looked at his face, relaxed and peaceful, and reassured herself. This handsome, caring man was her fiance, and she was worried about some internet camgirl?

"I love you, too," she whispered as she snuggled in closer.

Slowly, she drifted off to sleep for a second time that night.

Chapter Five

I found myself on the same street, just outside the piano shop. The seasons had changed it seemed, with a bright sun beaming down on the glossy green tree leaves. The store had a thin sheen of dust on the window, but through it, I could see that nothing had changed. The cat still sat at the grand piano, his paws poised over the keys. Something made me feel uncomfortable looking at it.

Was I dreaming again? The moment I had the thought, I could feel a tugging in my stomach and swirling in my head.

No. Nevermind. Of course it wasn't a dream.

Everything immediately settled.

I looked down at myself. I was wearing a short, yellow floral dress, something I would never wear. I had on pristine white canvas shoes that looked like they were fresh out of the box. I touched my head to find my hair pulled back behind a headband. The outfit seemed strange for me, but if I could accept the cat, I could work with this.

I began to wander down the sidewalk. Almost everything was coated in dust, not just the store windows; only the trees seemed to be untouched. It was as though the street had been abandoned for a hundred years. I saw a spark of yellow in a window and approached it. I reached my hand out and smudged some of the dust aside.

It was me, a mannequin me. It was wearing the same yellow dress and white shoes. The headband it wore was thick and black and the ponytail straight and looped low at the neck, not a style I wore. The mannequin was standing with a large, old book in the crook of its arm and a large flamboyant quill in its hand. As my eyes fell upon its face, my stomach sank. Its eyes were black and red, panic eyes, and tears were running down its cheeks.

I stumbled away from the window, my heart pounding. I felt as though I had seen something I was not meant to see. It seemed like it should be a secret, a dirty one, hidden deep down somewhere.

Trying to clear my mind of what I just witnessed, I turned the corner where the mouse had been and found myself on the same street I had started on. Thinking there had been a mistake, I headed down the same path, only to turn and be in the same spot again. Not knowing what else to do, I tried the door to the piano shop. It was locked, as was every other door on the street. I tried them all to no avail. I turned the corner and found myself standing in front of the pianos once more.

I started banging on the window and yelling for somebody to come out. Silence. I looked for a rock or a brick I could use to break it but came up with nothing. I started running. The stores looped past me, never changing. It was the same street over and over. I started to cry and ran faster. Just when I was about to fall to my knees and give up, something in a doorway caught my eye.

It was a pale blue bicycle with a broad white seat and knobby white handles. It was perfectly clean and shimmered in the ray of sunlight that fell on it.

I stopped and stared at it. It did not move or change. Slowly, I approached the bicycle. I was tense, waiting for something to happen, for it to roll away, for the yellow door behind it to swing open, for someone to appear behind me and caution against whatever I was about to do, but nothing happened. I grabbed one handle and tilted it up. It felt heavy and real. I nudged the kickstand up and wheeled it into the street. It glided easily beside me. As I swung my leg over the bar, I realized that the bicycle was perfectly adjusted to my height. I sent another glance towards the storefront, just to make sure nobody was there. Stillness. Silence.

I gingerly started to pedal. Everything was working as it should. The breeze blew my hair back and the sun began to warm my face. As I approached the end of the street, I could hear a piano playing softly in the distance.

Part of me wanted to stop to see where it was coming from, but my stomach twinged, telling me that something bad would come of it. I swallowed hard and pedaled faster, turning the corner.

As soon as I did, the scenery changed entirely. I was no longer on a quaint street, but in a sprawling neighborhood. The street had turned to cobblestone, worn down with grubby weeds straggling across the path. The buildings were made of a tan stone and red brick with dark roofs and crammed together haphazardly. They sat on hills and seemed to rise and fall in waves. Arches crossed the street overhead. Everything felt crowded and busy despite it being devoid of life. The music had grown louder, echoing inside my head.

Eventually the street narrowed, and I could very nearly reach both arms out and touch the buildings on either side of me. Ahead, I could see a tunnel and decided to continue on my path. As I crossed under, the music swelled. Inside, there were lights flickering and the tunnel seemed to split off into separate wings. For a brief moment, I thought I saw a shadow crossing a doorway, projected onto the opposite wall. It looked like a large man, holding something looped in his hand. I turned briefly towards it but could not stop the bike. It began to travel faster. I held on to the handlebars tightly, my knuckles turning white.

The tunnel opened up to a street similar to the one I had just been on, but this time, it was bustling with people. They all ignored me as I flew down the street. They were dressed very plainly, in all brown, and whispered amongst themselves. Some carried baskets over their arms, while others were pushing carts. I couldn't see what they were toting; it all looked like amorphous blobs of black and brown. The bicycle sped past them all, down into another tunnel.

This tunnel was the same as before, and I craned my neck to get a better look at the shadow on the wall. This time, the shadow had the loop raised in one hand, and a small figure in the other. The figure had longer hair, and the shadow of the man had its fist wrapped in it, lifting the figure up. As the other arm came down, I screamed. The small figure twisted and folded, but the man pulled it up by its hair and raised the other hand again. The piano music got louder. I yanked at the handlebars again, but they would not budge. I began to sob and screamed again.

"Let me go! Let me save her! Please!!"

The bicycle continued on its path, and soon we were back on the street. I yelled at the passersby, "Why won't you help her? She needs you!".

They all ignored me and continued carrying their things.

I slumped over the handlebars and cried. It was only a matter of minutes and we were back in the tunnel once more. I didn't want to look, but felt myself drawn. The figure had dropped the loop, but still held the smaller figure by the hair. As I watched, he walked across the doorway, then slammed the smaller figure's head into the door. I continued to watch the shadows on the wall, afraid to look at the actual doorway. Again and again, he pulled this figure's head back and smashed it into the door. At one point the figure raised an arm, pleadingly, but went limp shortly after. I gasped. I tried to get off the bike, but couldn't; it was as though my feet were glued to the pedals. It continued on its way. I did not bother calling out for help this time.

As I cried, we approached another tunnel. I begged not to go in, but the bike refused. We entered, and I took a deep breath. The lights flickered on and . . . nothing. All that was in the tunnel was a flight of stairs, which the bicycle promptly careened down. I held on even tighter and screamed. The bike bounced and darted this way and that as it tumbled down the stairs. The moment I hit level land, I let out a large sigh of relief. I tried again to leave the bicycle, and again, I was denied.

Once the tunnel was cleared, the road took on a slightly different look. These cobblestones were in good shape, there were no weeds, and the buildings had some space between them. There was a dead end up ahead with a tall building looming over the town. It was made of the same tan stone and red brick as the others, with stairs leading up to a large, wooden double door and wooden eaves and ledges capping off various levels. Most of the windows were dark, but there was a very large, open window at the top. A light shone through, highlighting stacks of papers and books. The piano music was the loudest it had been.

Suddenly, whatever had gripped the bicycle let go, and I stumbled off. I wheeled it up to the structure, nudged the kickstand down, and climbed up the steps. I straightened my dress and knocked on the door three times. I paused a moment. There was no answer. I knocked again, louder, and paused again. Still nothing. I tried opening it, but neither side would budge. I knew I needed to get up to that room, but how?

I stepped over to a window and tried to peer in. Curtains blocked my view. There was another window just above it. I carefully stepped on the sill, grabbed the ledge over it, and pulled myself up. This window was also closed off. I looked up; there were only a few more levels to go. I bolstered myself and began to climb. Everytime I looked up, it seemed the top was moving farther and farther away. I put my head down and listened to the music. In doing so, I fell into a sort of rhythm as I shimmied up the side of the building. The music seemed to encourage this, lifting and lilting in tune to something more wistful and pleasant.

Finally, my hand grabbed hold of a large ledge, and I heaved myself up over the edge. I turned and sat, staring out over the town. For as far as the eye could see, buildings stood in waves over hills and valleys. It was even more crowded than I had perceived on the street, and I could just barely see the people carrying their goods to and fro. I looked at the ledge I was sitting on and found myself surrounded by stacks of paper. As I went to grab one, the piano stopped and a voice rang out behind me.

"You can't touch that! Those haven't been filed yet!"

I turned. A young man stood in a white shirt and black vest. A red bow tie dangled, untied, around his neck. A piano sat to his left, presumably the one that had been playing this whole time.

"What are they?" I asked.

"Very important documents," he replied sternly.

"Well, can I help file them?" I asked.

He eyed me suspiciously and smoothed the dark hair on the back of his head.

"I don't believe you could handle the task appropriately," he answered, pulling in his already gaunt cheeks.

I crawled off the ledge and into the room with him. He was a little taller than I was, but he was noticeably younger. I assessed the situation and decided I could probably intimidate him and get my way.

As I had the thought, he smirked. "Don't even try it. These papers are not for you. If you insist on snooping, I do have a few things for you to review, if you would like."

I was taken aback. Did he know what I was going to try to do? How?

He shook his head. "You are a little dense, lord bless. Follow me."

I nodded my head sheepishly and began to follow him into the next room. Whereas the old room had been ornate and lit in a warm, glowing orange light, this room was stark. Filing cabinets lined the walls, and a singular recliner sat in the middle of the room.

The young man gestured around. "Any filing cabinet that is open, you may explore to your heart's content."

"And the locked ones?" I asked.

He smiled. "Those are for a later date."

"Will I come back to this place later, then?"

He chuckled a little. "You can come back anytime you like. You just have to find the window."

That seems reasonable, I thought. I looked at all the cabinets. They were all the same shade of light grey and stood about six feet tall. There were no labels on any of them, so I chose one at random. Locked.

The next one was locked, too, but the third time proved to be the charm.

The files were labeled in a language I didn't understand. I pulled a sheet out from one and stared at it. There were no words to be read, just three dripping dots, but suddenly, I was in a different place. I was in my childhood bedroom. My small, wooden bed was on one side of the room, and my brother's crib was on the other. On my bed were layers of stuffed animals.

I watched as a young blonde girl, a young me, no older than four, stormed into the room.

"I hate the floor, I hate the walls, I hate you, and I hate these stupid toys."

With that she began flinging stuffed animals around the room. She let out a primal scream as she ripped the blankets off the bed. From just outside the room came a loud sobbing. The girl stood there glaring, teeth gritted for a moment. Then, her face fell. She stood a moment staring blankly at her bed, then blinked and darted back out of the room.

"Mommy, don't cry, I don't hate you. Mommy, I love you. I love you, Mommy. I'll fix it. See?"

She ran back in and started to make the bed. She placed the animals on the bed haphazardly, with the grace and finesse of a four year old. Some kept tumbling off, and she began to cry, too.

"I'll fix it, Mommy, I'll fix it. I'm sorry. I'm sorry I'm bad. I'm sorry."

Suddenly I was jolted back into the filing room. My face was wet with tears, and my body was trembling. The young man looked at me with a raised eyebrow.

"Find a rough one, hmm?"

"I don't feel so good," I croaked out.

He led me to the recliner and helped me sit down. I started to sob. He rubbed my shoulders and hair while I did.

"There, there," he said reassuringly, "You're going to be okay. This is over. It was just a piece of time. You've already lived it. There's no going back; it's just a couple of pages in one big novel."

This made me cry harder.

He knelt beside me.

"Why don't you wake up, forget all about this?"

I thought about it a moment, then nodded weakly.

"Alright, let's do it together, Samantha."

He grabbed my hand.

"What's your name?" I asked.

He shook his head and smiled. "Time to wake up. Count of three. One. Two. Thr-"

Chapter Six

Samantha woke up and stretched her arms. She peeked at her phone: 5:42 am.

She settled back into bed. There were still a few minutes before she would have to get up and start loading luggage into the car. Rob, true to his nature, was still passed out beside her, curled up into a ball with his arms crossed over his chest. She snuggled her face into a pillow, letting the remnants of her dream swirl in her head.

She couldn't remember much past riding a bicycle and hearing her mother cry. There was something about a young man with pale skin and dark hair, too. Maybe he was the reason she was crying? Samantha felt she had always had a good relationship with her mom, except for some butting heads in her teen years.

She flipped over to her side and stared at Rob. His hair was sticking up over his ear, and his mouth was hanging open. Every so often, he would emit a drawn out snore, complete with a small snort at the end. His hands were balled into fists as if ready to take on some unseen foe.

Samantha smiled to herself. He was cute when he slept. She rarely got to see him fall asleep, going to bed far earlier than he did, but she did love waking up to him sleeping next to her. He was always so peaceful, never thrashing around or screaming, as she did sometimes. He refused to sleep more than six hours at a time, though, a practice that worried her. He insisted any longer would make him sluggish and useless all day. He often only got four hours of sleep a night, but still made it through the day unscathed. Samantha envied him. Eight hours never seemed enough, but she knew, logically, that twelve hours were far too many.

As she stared, his eyes fluttered open. He jumped a little.

"Holy shit, Sam, you scared the crap out of me."

"I'm just creeping on you," she replied, sliding closer to him. "Is it illegal to creep on my fiance?"

He rubbed his eyes and blinked at her. "It's too early to be creeping."

"When did you get back to bed?" she asked.

"Mmm, around two," he replied.

She pushed his arm. "Dude! We have a long ways to drive today. Are you going to be able to make it?"

Rob rolled over. "Of course. I'll be fine."

There was a moment of silence, followed by a soft snoring.

Samantha shifted over onto her back and grabbed her phone again. She reset her alarm for 6:30 and began to scroll through her social media pages. There were a ton of posts from airports, people toasting each other at small cafes, sneak peeks of the convention set up from some of the developers and vendors. Rob was tagged in a number of posts expressing desire to see him and grab a beer or two. They were mostly from men, other streamers and game developers, but there were a few women, as well. Samantha opened up their profiles and scrolled through briefly. One was an artist for a studio in Australia. She seemed quiet and nerdy. Another was a model from England, but all of her pictures included her boyfriend. One by one, Samantha screened them for any sense of a threat, but found nothing. This pleased her.

Maybe I'm getting better about all of this, she thought.

"Yes!" said a supportive voice. "You are beautiful and worthy, and those other women are just regular people."

You're right, she thought. These women were not threats. They wanted to check out the games and the people who were going to be there. Their lives had no impact on hers, and Rob wasn't that kind of guy anyway. They were just ordinary other people.

Happy with this revelation, she closed out of social media and went to the event page. She checked out which studios were going to be there, who the vendors were, and what panels were taking place. There were a number of panels about psychology and self improvement. She made a mental note to check those out while she was there. Psychology always fascinated her, though she gave therapists a wide berth. She had a gut feeling they would diagnose her with ultimate crazy and send her away somewhere. No, she was doing just fine on her own, and she could only do better the more she learned.

"You're going to learn so much!" the voice said. "And you'll meet so many interesting people! They're all going to love you!"

Samantha thought about it. Of course they would. What wasn't to love? She was smart, funny, and probably a better gamer than her fiance. All she would have to do is crack a few jokes, toss back a few beers, and she would be well on her way as everyone's favorite. Favorite what, though? She thought for a moment. She could start streaming, too. She could stream herself gaming or doing art or singing. She would need to pick up some sketchbooks, if that were the case, and maybe some cute outfits. Nothing low cut, of course; she would have a classy stream, one that would be taken seriously and become a worldwide sensation.

She laid there, her thoughts racing about all the possible outcomes. Perhaps she had found a purpose! She had attempted to stream before, around the time Rob started. She had burned out pretty quickly, but this would be different. She was determined now, and she was going to buck up and network so hard at the convention.

Samantha looked down at her nails. No way would those work. They would have to stop by the store before they left so she could get some fake ones. She would also need to get some false lashes to highlight her eyes.

She got out of bed and went to the living room where the luggage was. She opened her bag and began to sort through it.

No, none of this will work, she thought. She ran to the closet and began to pull out new shirts and dresses, flowier, showier outfits. She stuffed those into the suitcase and added a couple of stilettos to it. She began to wonder if the red dress was going to be swanky enough, but dismissed the thought.

As she zipped the bag back up, a voice ran through her head.

"Are you okay? This seems a little much," it said.

"Of course she's okay!" the supportive voice cried. "She's the best!"

"Maybe you should sit down and take a breath," the concerned voice continued. "You don't want to overwhelm yourself."

Samantha ignored it. She didn't have time to deal with uneasy voices. She was finally at a high point, and she was going to enjoy it.

"Hair spray!" the supportive voice interjected. "Purple hairspray!"

"Yes!" Samantha said out loud. "Hairspray, nails, lashes, yes!"

Her alarm went off, and she jumped a little. She shut it off, returned to the bedroom, and threw on some clothes. Rob was still asleep, but that was fine with her. She snuck out the door and got into her car.

She didn't remember much of the ride there, but brushed it off as excitement over the trip. She pulled up to a cosmetics store and ran inside. She couldn't find the hairspray but did find some purple gel. She went into the next aisle and stared at the rack of lashes. She couldn't decide between full, plush ones and a long, dramatic set, so she grabbed both. She turned around and found herself looking at the nails. There were the basic French manicured sets, but she had no interest in those. Most of the clothes she was going to wear were black, and there was a set of long, pointed nails dipped in silver glitter. They were perfect. She also picked up a set of cherry red nails to wear with her dress.

As she was walking towards the checkout, she spotted a tube of gorgeously dark red lipstick. She looked at the price- $50. She thought for a moment. This trip was expensive, and they were a little tight on funds as it was. Should she really make that purchase?

"How long does lipstick last?" asked the supportive voice. "It's a long term investment! You're going to love it and use it all the time!"

Right, Samantha thought, the new sexy, confident me would definitely rock that lipstick.

She popped it into the basket and stepped in line. When the older lady at the register rang up the total, she flinched for a moment, but that same voice popped up encouraging her.

On the way home, it continued to give her a pep talk. It wasn't just her that would be benefiting from this, but her fiance, too! It wouldn't be fair to him to see all of the other streamers with beautiful women hanging on their every word if he didn't have someone gorgeous with him, too.

"Well, I'm sure Cassie would be happy to," a wheedling voice started.

Samantha blocked it out. Cassie was trash. This was Samantha's time to shine.

She skipped into the apartment and found Rob sitting at the kitchen table. He looked at her sleepily.

"Where'd you go?" he asked.

Samantha held up her bag. "Shopping! I needed some stuff for the convention."

Rob's eyes widened. "Oh, okay. Cool."

Samantha tilted her head. "What?" she asked.

Rob shook his head. "Nothing, it's just. Well. I kind of thought you were going to cancel last minute. You know, stay home, game a little, catch up on sleep. You didn't seem like you were crazy excited over going."

Samantha smiled and walked over to him. She gave him a big kiss on the top of the head. "Of course I am! Now, I need to get ready before we go."

She trotted off towards the bedroom.

"Do you want breakfast?" Rob called after her.

"No, thanks," she replied, "not hungry!"

She pulled on a tight pair of skinny jeans and laced up some short black boots over them. She dug in her closet until she found a faded black band tee that fell off her shoulder. She pulled it on and modeled it in front of the mirror. It was loose enough to flow, but tight enough to show off a bit of her figure. Perfect. She ran into the bathroom.

She straightened her hair and ran the purple gel through a strip of it before pulling it into a high ponytail. She applied the lashes with some difficulty, probably using too much glue, then finished her makeup. Last, but not least, she began to apply the nails.

Rob wandered in to brush his teeth. He stopped and stared.

"Yes?" Samantha asked.

He shook his head. "Nothing. It's just like you're a whole different person."

"That good, huh?" she asked teasingly.

Rob grinned. "Very good."

They finished getting ready and went to load up the luggage.

"Ooooh, I'm sorry, Rob," Samantha said. She clicked her nails together. "Don't think I can do it with these talons."

Rob sighed and gave her a tired look. She smiled innocently back.

He packed the car, while she went through the apartment, unplugging things and turning off lights.

When I come back, she thought, things will be so much better.

They got into the car, Rob in the driver's seat, and took off. This trip was going to be a solid nine hour drive.

"Do you think we'll make it in time to grab dinner with people?"

Rob glanced at Samantha, a hesitant look on his face.

"We should," he said, "but are you sure you want to eat with people? I figured you would be a bit worn out after the trip."

Samantha waved her hand at him. "I'll be fine," she said. "Besides, it will let you hang out with your friends a little more."

Rob gave her a big smile. "True. Also, our friends. Our."

Something twinged inside of Samantha, but she buried it down. "Of course," she smiled. "Our friends."

The road trip was fun, as they usually were. Samantha played dj and kept the banter with Rob up. They talked a little bit about the convention, but also found themselves debating the merits of various games and riffs on the small towns they were passing by. They stopped at a gas station at one point and bought an enormous amount of snacks- chips, candy bars, cookies, pastries, jerky, soda. Lunch was a quick fast food taco stop. This trip was not going to be health conscious at all.

About an hour away from their destination, Samantha started messaging people about dinner plans. She got a yes from Jason and Todd; they had just arrived at their suite a block down. Another friend of theirs, Cameron, said he would be there with his wife, Sarah. Everyone else was arriving later or already had plans.

As they pulled up to the building, Samantha gasped. It was a cute little townhouse with a wrought iron gate and dark blue shutters.

"How did you find this place?" she asked Rob.

He grinned and shrugged. "I have my sources."

They retrieved a key from the pin code lock box on the door and stepped inside. The wooden floors were old and worn. The living room had a big dark leather couch and large television hanging on the wall. Rob had packed his console, so they were definitely going to have guests. The kitchen was small, but very charming, with striped curtains and a large archway looking into the living room. Rob went outside to grab their luggage, while Samantha went upstairs.

The entire bedroom was filled with a king sized bed. There was a little space to go to the balcony and another aisle leading to the bathroom. True to Rob's word, the tub was huge. There was a detachable shower head above it, but Samantha wasn't sure she was going to use it all that often. No, she was going to soak in bubbles, lots and lots of bubbles.

"I love it!" she called down to Rob.

"Good!" he yelled back. "Can I get a hand?"

She peeked down the stairs at him. He looked up at her wearily. She clacked her nails.

"Sorry. I would if I could."

Rob groaned. Samantha smirked. "Should have gotten more sleep!"

He got the suitcases upstairs, and Samantha began to help him unpack.

"When did you pack this?" Rob asked, holding up a flimsy black top.

"This morning," Samantha replied. "I figured it would be good in case we go out to a bar or something."

He eyed her carefully. "Are you sure you're feeling okay?" he asked.

Samantha shoved him playfully. "I am perfectly fine. Just excited about this convention!"

Rob shrugged and continued to unpack.

When they were done, Samantha touched up her hair and makeup, and they hopped back into the car. They were going to a casual Italian place. When they arrived, everyone was waiting outside.

"SAM!" Sarah screamed and ran over to hug her.

"SARAH!" Samantha called back. They embraced.

"How have you been?" Sarah asked. "You look so good!"

"Oh, you know," Samantha replied, "busy, but good. How about you?"

Sarah laughed. "Girl, do I have stories to tell you."

Jason and Todd stepped away from Rob, and each gave Samantha a "bro hug"- two quick pats on the back.

"Sam," they each said.

"Nice to see you guys," she replied.

Jason looked exhausted, but Todd was beaming ear to ear. "Good to see you, too," he said.

Cameron stubbed out his cigarette and waved at everyone. "I don't know about you, but I am starving. Let's grab some food!"

They all clambered into the restaurant and were seated at a large table in the corner.

"Should we just do pizza?" Rob asked, looking over the menu.

"No way," Cameron replied. "You're going to turn into a pizza one of these days. Let's try something a bit more sophisticated."

"So, spaghetti and meatballs?" Todd retorted.

Cameron shrugged, "Whatever goes well with the lager I'm getting."

Samantha paused internally for a moment. What would cool, confident her order to drink? Was beer beneath her? Wine too cliche?

"Rum and coke!" the funny voice, Eric, said.

Samantha smiled. Rum and coke it would be.

They all ordered and the first round of drinks arrived. Samantha's was stronger than she was expecting, but she kept her cool.

Rob was making a show of his personal pizza, and Cameron was lecturing him on getting variety in his diet, while waving a calzone at him. Todd and Jason were catching up with Sarah about her kids. Samantha was left to sip her drink in silence.

The waitress swung by and asked if she would like a refill. "Yes, please!" Samantha cried.

As the second one went down, she could feel the blood rushing to her face. Jason caught her eye and winked at her, raising his beer a bit. Samantha winked back and raised her glass in response. She was just at the right point of tipsy. She reached across the table and snatched Todd's hat off his head.

"Hey, give it back," he exclaimed, grabbing at it.

"No!" she replied, "It's rude. No hats inside."

Todd launched himself over the table, and Samantha passed the hat to Sarah.

Sarah put it on and modeled it briefly, before passing it on to Cameron.

"Bro, why do you even wear these?" he asked, examining the hat carefully. "It's not like your hair is thinning."

"It's to keep all those voices he hears quiet," Jason responded in a spooky voice, wiggling his fingers. "They don't bug him with the hat on."

Todd snatched it back from Cameron. "Very funny," he said. "I just happen to look good in a hat, and you're jealous because you don't!"

The waitress came by again. Everyone ordered dessert, and Samantha had one last rum and coke. The world seemed to adopt a different rhythm, pulsing at the edges slightly. She felt as though she owned it all, and nothing could take her down. She began to regale her dinner companions with all sorts of stories, tales about Rob, playthroughs of video games, ideas for her stream, any topic that caught her fancy.

At one point Todd made a mildly suggestive joke, and Samantha found herself cackling at it. Everyone at the table gave her a sideways look, and suddenly, her whole cool facade slipped. They were judging her; she was drunk, and they were judging her. The impact was akin to a baseball breaking a window.

While everyone split the check and made plans to meet up in the morning, she sank down in her chair. What was she thinking, talking on and on like that? And these stupid nails, why did she buy them? She couldn't pick anything up, she had made Rob do all the lifting. Why? So she could look nice? Since when did that ever happen?

"Never. When have you ever looked nice? Nails can't fix a whole pig," a thin voice piped up.

Everyone gathered their things and made their way outside. Rob gently held a hand to Samantha's back the whole time.

It's because I'm a useless drunk, she thought. He's probably mortified.

More hugs went around, and the group split up into their separate cars. Rob drove and was quiet the whole time.

As they pulled up to the house, Samantha asked in a tiny, shaky voice, "Did I do okay?"

Rob looked at her like one would look at a stampeding bull. "Of course you did. Did you have fun?"

Samantha nodded quietly, fighting the tears that were coming up. She had been having a good time, until she remembered who she was.

They went inside, and Samantha immediately ran upstairs. She looked in the mirror. The shirt was too tight across her chest and you could see the muffin top the skinny jeans had squeezed out..

She looked at the nails and purple streak in her hair. What was this nonsense? She looked like a try hard middle schooler.

She burst into tears and began to rip the nails off. It hurt and left residue on her natural nails, but she felt immensely better after they were off. She peeled off her clothes and lashes and turned on the showerhead. The bubble bath would have to wait.

Samantha began to methodically scrub her whole body while watching the purple gel swirl down the drain.

"Stupid girl," the thin voice spoke up. "Stupid, fat, ugly girl."

Samantha cried and scrubbed harder. The nails and lashes, all of those purchases, they were all a waste. How could she have thought that this trip would be a good idea?

"Not just the trip, but the dinner," it continued. "You made such a fool of yourself. How can you ever trust yourself in public knowing what you are?"

She nodded and felt her jaw tremble. It was true. They had even made a point about hearing voices, and here she was, hearing voices. She was weird, a freak, crazy. They were all cool and collected. They would be at ease surrounded by all those beautiful people tomorrow. Nothing would phase them the way it did her. What was wrong with her?

Suddenly, from outside the shower, Rob's voice rang out.

"Hey, are you still cool with the cafe for breakfast tomorrow?" he asked.

Samantha swallowed and tried to keep her voice level.

"Uh, sure. That sounds good."

"Okay, just checking," he said. "You've been in there awhile, so I wasn't sure if you were feeling okay."

Samantha instinctively turned the shower off. She rubbed her eyes one last time and opened the curtain.

Rob smiled and handed her a towel. As she reached for it, he frowned.

"What happened to your nails?" he asked.

She blinked. "I got tired of them," she replied. "I couldn't really do anything with them on, so I took them off."

"You were so excited to have them," he said. "Are you sure?"

"Oh, yeah. There's more glue in the bag, so I can put them back on later. No biggie."

She wrapped herself up in the towel and stepped out of the shower. She stumbled a little.

Rob caught her and laughed.

"Easy, drunky," he teased.

Samantha's face flushed. She was out of control, even Rob could see that.

"I think I just need to go to bed," she mumbled.

"That's probably a good idea," he replied, pushing a wet strand of hair out of her face. "You were tossing and turning last night when I got to bed, and tomorrow's going to be a crazy day."

Samantha nodded quietly.

"I would join you," he continued, "but a few of the guys are jumping into a server, so I'm going to meet up with them for a bit. I also need to make a few posts to let people know what I'm up to."

He gave her a big kiss and smiled at her.

"Beautiful drunky," he said.

Samantha's lip started to tremble, but she caught it.

"Love you," she replied.

"Love you, too" he called out, already turned around and heading for the stairs.

Samantha stumbled over to the bed and fell into it. Her whole body began to wrack with sobs. While Rob carried on with his friends, she cried. The voices were a swirl at this point, barely intelligible over one another. Not all of them were mean, but the mean ones were the loudest. Eventually, they quieted, and Samantha's crying ebbed into sniffling.

She rolled over and grabbed her phone. Multiple notifications lit up the screen.

One glowed bright blue: "Robket_Ship has tagged you in a photo!"

Samantha groaned but opened it anyway. It was a picture of the six of them around the dinner table. Everyone was looking at the camera and smiling except Samantha. She had her mouth open, mid sentence and half-empty glass of rum and coke in her hand. Her eyes were closed, and her face was red. Sure enough, she was all boobs, belly rolls, and double chins.

The comments had already started rolling in. Most of them were in excitement over seeing people in person, but more than a few were about her.

"Wow, Sam is enjoying herself!"

"As for Sam, get it girl!!!"

"Alright, who gave Sam the booze?"

"Cool to see Robket and the crew, but who's the drunk obnoxious chick in the back?"

"Know your limits, kids, or you'll end up like this."

"Poor Rob had to roll her home, I bet."

Samantha threw her phone onto the nightstand and cried a little more. Slowly she drifted off to sleep, tear-stained face buried in a pillow.

Chapter Seven

The sound of the bell ringing jerked me awake. I could feel the sore spot on my head where it had been resting on the desk I was sitting at. I rubbed at it with the back of my hand and looked myself over.

I was in a ratty pair of threadbare jeans and a thin band tee. My hoodie had holes ripped in the sleeves for my thumbs and was starting to split around the seams. I blushed and looked around at everyone else in the class. They were dressed to the nines, in cute dresses, skirts, flowing tops, slacks, and polos. I knew without looking that rather than the flawless, on point makeup I saw on the faces around me, I was peering out at the world through racoon-rimmed eyes. This was definitely high school.

The teacher in the front of the room, Ms. Shirley, underscored an item she had written on the board.

"If you get through your reading early, I want you to start on your life essays," she said, turning to look at us. She was a petite woman with curling black hair, and she held the class captive. Nobody dared speak when she was in the room. Rumors abound that she was a witch, an actual witch.

"Are there any questions?" she asked.

When nobody replied, she gave the class a curt nod and moved to her desk.

A few people stood up gathering their books, and I felt a wave of panic. Was the bell for the class to start or end? I looked around, confused, and saw some people pulling out notebooks and pencils. I reached under my desk and felt around in the tray. There was nothing there. I looked around my desk, but I didn't see my backpack anywhere. More people began to trickle out, leaving only a handful behind. Those who did stay were furiously writing in notebooks, flipping the finished pages over frantically.

"Ms. Little!"

I jumped and looked ahead. Ms. Shirley was now standing in front of me, arms crossed sternly. I had only looked around for a moment. How had she moved so quickly?

"What do you think you are doing?"

"I'm just . . . I . . . you see," I began to stammer.

The pages fell silent, and everyone stared at me. A few more stood and stepped out into the hallway.

"I was just going to go to my locker," I said, hoping this was the right answer.

"Why didn't you go before class?" Ms. Shirley replied. It was not the right answer. I looked around only to find every desk occupied. It was as if no one had left.

"She was too busy sleeping, Ms. Shirley," a thin, reedy voice chimed in.

I turned to see a heavy set girl with chin-length red hair and freckles in a collared sweater pointing her finger at me.

"You know how spacey she is," she continued, sneering at me. "She probably doesn't even know where she is right now. What an airhead!"

"No!" I shouted, "I promise, I just-"

"I saw it myself," she said. "She was passed out drooling on her desk like some disgusting animal. Gross!"

The class began to giggle and whisper. My eyes darted over them, trying to spot a friend in the crowd and finding none. They all mirrored the red head, sneering and pointing at me. I looked up at Ms. Shirley. She glared down at me and raised a hand into the air. The class fell silent again.

"Well, Ms. Little, if you are taking the time to rest, then surely your essay is done. Why don't you present it to the class?"

I swallowed hard and looked down at my desk. Suddenly, there was a stack of papers in front of me. They were all covered in my handwriting. I reached out and picked up a page; the tips of my fingers were stained with ink. I read the first line- "my life essay- a dissertation on despair".

"In front of the class, Ms. Little," she said harshly.

I jumped out of the desk and grabbed at the stack of papers, only to have them scatter all around me. Everyone began to laugh again, and I dropped to my knees in tears.

As I cried and gathered up the sheets, I heard the same girl mocking me.

"What a freaking clutz. Seriously, how does she even get through the day? If I were that graceful, I'd trip myself off a cliff just to end it all."

I lifted up my desk a bit to free a page trapped under one of the legs. The girl let out a harsh laugh.

"Oooooh, so strong! How can someone so fat be that strong? She's like an ogre!"

The class howled in laughter. I spotted a page laying on the bookcase next to the mouse cage. I stumbled over towards it.

The mouse watched me as I snatched it up, its little white paws combing through its whiskers. I stopped a moment and stared back at it. Something about the mouse bothered me. Its dark red eyes bore into my soul.

"Ummm, are you seriously trying to win a staring contest with a mouse? Weirdo!"

The voice brought me back to the scene. Ms. Shirley sharply pointed her finger to the podium at the front of the classroom. The red haired girl leered at me as I walked up to it, clutching my pages to my chest.

"Umm, so, my essay," I started, spreading the pages out in front of me. The words swam around on the pages, staying just out of my sight. I traced them with my finger, trying to slow them down or stop them from moving altogether. They ducked and danced around my fingertip, the ink swirling from my hand onto the page, adding to their motion.

"Now, Ms. Little," Ms. Shirley barked.

My breathing was rapid, my heart beating out of my chest. I felt ice cold and flushed at the same time. The class was still laughing at me as teardrops fell down my face. One splashed onto the page and trapped a single line.

"My life essay," I read aloud, "a discussion of desperation."

No, that wasn't right. The words swam in the tear for a moment, then refocused.

"My life essay," I read again, "a discourse on despondency."

That still wasn't right. I anxiously flipped through the pages some more, but they were all blank. I turned back to the first page and watched as straggling drops of ink crawled to the center of the page. They came together and formed one large word in block letters.

RUN.

"What are you looking at, Ms. Little?"

I glanced up, and my heart stopped for a moment.

Ms. Shirley and the class all grinned at me, their jaws intermittently lolling open into rolling grimaces. Their eyes were black and swirling with red. The panic eyes were back.

"You should run; now."

The familiar voice came from the door to my right. It was the redhead. She wasn't sneering at me anymore and even looked a bit frightened herself. Her eyes were normal and set into a serious, deadpan expression.

"Now!" she yelled before running down the hallway.

The screech of chairs rang out as my classmates stood up. I threw the podium over towards Ms. Shirley and chased after the girl. I caught sight of the hem of her skirt just as it disappeared around a corner. I turned down the same corridor and saw her veer left into another hallway. We continued like this for several more lengths, followed by screams and gales of laughter. Doors around us began to fling open, and others came pouring out into the halls, joining the chaos. They all had the panic eyes, too. As they amassed, I could feel the energy of the larger sickness as a whole. It seemed to gather itself into its own being, a monster in its own right, and began to hunt me down.

"Over here!"

I stopped and peered down the passage. The girl held a glass door open.

"Are you kidding me? Don't stop, you idiot, get over here!"

I stumbled over and through the door. I ran down the concrete steps, and fell into the grass below. I looked up just as bodies began to hit the door. They grinned at me, pressing against the glass. The girl sighed and began to make her way down the stairs.

"We have to keep running," I cried, scrambling to my feet.

"Nah," she said as she waved a hand dismissively. "They can't get out."

I looked back at the door and saw that the figures were gone.

"Well, that was fun while it lasted. Why do you always ruin everything?" the girl asked.

I stammered. "What do you mean? What was that? Why does it always happen?"

She shrugged. "Ask your stupid mouse friend."

"Mouse friend? What?"

She turned and shook a finger in my face. "You're fucked up. You have to know that. You're fat and stupid and useless and, to top it all off, batshit crazy. You're doing this to yourself."

"Charity!!"

We both spun around. A woman was walking up to us. She was short, with a head full of dark brown ringlets. As she approached, her coppery brown eyes flashed at the redhead.

"That is enough," she continued. "You don't say another word."

"What do you want, Ariana?" Charity asked, rolling her eyes.

"I'm here to fix this," she answered. She looked me over with concern. "Are you okay?"

I nodded, thoroughly confused. Ariana turned to Charity.

"We will talk about this later," she said sternly, "but for now, we have to get her out of here."

"Everything is under control," Charity replied. "Stop being so overdramatic."

"No, you've had your fun. This has gotten way out of hand," Ariana retorted.

She turned back to me. "Do you remember the trick I taught you when you were younger? How to wake up?"

I nodded.

"Good," she said, relieved. "I need you to do that."

I shook my head. "I think it's fine now," I replied. "They're gone, and I want to know what she meant by the mouse."

Ariana placed a hand on my shoulder. "It's not safe," she stated. "You need to wake up."

"No!" I responded. "I'm tired of this. What are those people? Why do they have the panic eyes? Why does it feel like another creature is with them? What is it about the mouse?"

Charity smirked. "She wants answers. You've been coddling her. No wonder she's so soft."

Ariana held her other hand up to silence her and gripped my shoulder tightly.

"This isn't the way to do it. Trust me. Right now, if you don't get out of here, they will find you again."

"Who? Why?" I demanded.

"Yeah, why?" Charity repeated mockingly.

"Shut up," Ariana snipped back. "You aren't helping anyone, as usual."

"I help plenty!" Charity cried out. "You're just so obsessed with yourself you can't see that. No wonder Eric stopped hanging out with you, you bitch!"

I blinked. Eric?

Ariana let go of my shoulder and focused all of her attention on Charity. They began to argue back and forth. I used the opportunity to run away from them. I crossed the school lawn, darted past the cars in the parking lot, and headed for a tunnel next to a large church. I thought I heard someone call my name but continued to run.

The tunnel was dark and ran with a foot of water. I splashed through it, feeling the cold sludge soak into my sneakers. I heard my name again and pushed myself to run faster. The tunnel was swimming with shadows and shrieks. I felt deeply that this was a dangerous place and focused on the light at the end. As I burst through the exit, I could have sworn I felt someone grab at my hair. The streets I found myself on were made of cobblestone, and the buildings were heaped up on top of one another. They seemed to narrow and tighten in on me as I made my way deeper into the town.

As I ran, I heard footsteps behind me. I looked back, expecting to see one or both of them chasing after me. There was nobody there. I turned my head and heard a screaming laugh echo out into the street. Ariana was right, they were going to find me again.

These streets were very familiar, though, and I felt a surge of confidence hit me. If I kept going, I thought, I would come to a dead end. Sure enough, a few minutes later, I did. A towering building loomed over me, the sound of piano music lilting through the cacophony of laughter and screaming behind me.

I hiked my foot up onto the first windowsill and started to scale the building. As I went to push off, a hand wrapped around my ankle.

I looked down and finally saw it: a huge crowd of people filling the streets, all with panic eyes, all staring at me. I screamed and kicked at the hand that grabbed me. It let go, and I continued to climb. They shrieked in anger and pounded on the wall. I could feel the larger presence phasing over the crowd, aiming for me. I scrambled up faster.

Just as I knew if I looked over my shoulder, I was done, I felt another hand grab onto my hoodie and yank me up over the edge of the roof.

"Get in," the young man cried, ushering me over stacks of papers.

I did as he said, and he slammed the window closed behind me, shoving a large, rusty deadbolt into place. I heard a roaring noise brush against the glass, then dissipate.

"This is a mess," the man said, running his fingers through his hair. "Where is Ariana?"

I reached for a file sitting on the edge of the piano.

"Don't touch that!" he snapped.

I raised my hands up defensively. He shook his head and sighed.

"Why didn't you wake up?" he asked.

"I had questions," I replied quietly.

"We all have questions!" he shouted back at me. "It isn't an excuse to endanger the system, though!"

"I . . . I just wanted to know," I stuttered.

"What?" he interrupted. "What did you want to know? Because there isn't a whole lot for me to tell you."

"But you have all these files," I pointed out.

"And they are not for you," he reiterated. "You have to figure some things out for yourself."

I stared at him inquisitively.

"How should I go about that, then?" I asked.

He looked at me, startled. He didn't have to tell me, though. I knew by his expression.

"You don't know," I said. "You don't have a clue what any of this is."

"Oh, and you think Charity does?" he retorted.

"Yes, I do," I replied.

"All she knows is your faults," he said sharply. "She can call you out on every little thing all day long, but in the end, she knows just as much as the rest of us."

I could tell he was being sincere. She had said a number of hurtful things, and her voice was identical to the one that berated me day in and day out. Something bothered me, though, about his response. I couldn't put my finger on it, until I looked around.

The room seemingly had no doors. There was an archway leading into a file room, but no entrance, no exit, just a large, half-circle window. I turned back to him.

He stared at me silently, chewing the inside of his cheek.

"What?" he asked.

"How do you know about that?" I asked.

"Know what?" he snarled.

"That I talked to Charity? Or that Ariana told me to wake up? How do you know these things? This room is sealed off. You can't have been there."

He shook his head. "No. I'm not getting into this with you."

He lifted his hand up to me as I cried out, "What is going o-"

Chapter Eight

Samantha's eyes fluttered open. The light blue of the wall filled her eyes. She rolled over onto her back and looked at the flat expanse of the ceiling. For a moment her mind raced. Where was she? Wherever it was, it was better than where she usually woke up. This calmed her a bit, and she turned to the other side of the bed.

It was empty and the sheets were ruffled up. A shower was running in the distance. Slowly, she began to piece together the past couple of days. As she realized how she had acted, she groaned and pulled the blanket up over her head. Why did she think she could suddenly be this social butterfly in the center of everyone's attention?

"Oh no," she whispered. "Oh no."

She had told all their friends that she was going to start her own stream. Maybe they had brushed it off or forgotten about it. She couldn't stream. She didn't have the time or energy. Her breathing became shallow, and her face grew hot. She pulled the blanket tighter.

"What have I done?" she muttered.

"What didn't you do, stupid girl," a spindly voice answered. "You made a fool of yourself in front of your friends! You spent all that money on trash! You drank too much and now everyone hates you!"

"She only had a few drinks," a stronger, soothing voice replied. "Barely tipped her over."

"They don't hate her," another laid back voice responded. "Nobody hates her. Get out of here."

Samantha nodded. Maybe they were right.

She pulled the blanket off her head. The shower was still running. Rob, once again, must have only had four hours of sleep. Knowing him, he would want food and lots of it. She couldn't remember if they had made plans for breakfast, so she picked up her phone. It was blowing up with notifications. Her stomach dropped. Right. The social media comments.

"I told you," the stringy voice piped up again. "Everyone hates you!"

Samantha groaned. She didn't really want to go out now.

"Oh, but you have to," the voice said mockingly. "You promised you would. Besides, it's entertainment for them. Let's see what stupid thing you do next! Will you get plastered and spew emotions all over people? Will you say something stupid and insensitive and watch everyone's skin crawl? The possibilities are endless with you!"

The shower stopped, and a few minutes later, Rob came into the room.

"Good morning, drunky," he said chipperly. "How are you feeling?"

Samantha panicked for a moment. She couldn't tell him how she really felt; it would bring his whole day down. Would he be able to tell she was lying?

"I'm good," she answered. hesitantly "Just a little tired."

He shook his head. "I still don't understand how you don't get hangovers."

Samantha shrugged, "It was only a few drinks, barely tipped me over."

Rob started to pull a shirt on. "Hey, it would've knocked me on my ass."

As Rob got dressed and moved around the room, Samantha stared blankly at her phone. She didn't dare open all the notifications.

"Just because you don't look, it doesn't mean they're not there," the voice reminded her in a sing-song tone.

"Um, Samantha," Rob said.

Samantha jumped and looked up. He was standing next to the bed staring down at her. He was dressed in his traditional streaming attire- long sleeve button up, grey vest, and the loudest basketball shorts he could find. His whole schtick was that the Robket was all party below decks. His convention passes hung from a galaxy printed lanyard around his neck, and he had a backpack slung over his shoulder.

"Yes?" she replied.

"You've been in bed all morning. You haven't moved since I got out of the shower. Are you sure you're okay?"

Samantha shook her head. "Of course," she said, "I'm just a little tired is all."

"He knows," the thin voice whispered again. "He knows. You just ruined everything. He knows you're a blubbering, blithering mess. You've ruined his day with all your moping."

Rob smiled reassuringly. "No worries; we'll get you some coffee at the cafe."

The cafe! Samantha remembered. They were meeting friends at the cafe.

"Shit," she said and began to dart around the room.

"Don't tell me you forgot," Rob groaned.

"Nope," she said, "nope, nope, nope." She dug through her clothes. "Maybe a little," she admitted.

"Well, we've still got a little bit of time," Rob said. "Just jump into something cute, and we'll head out."

That was the struggle Samantha was having. All the clothes she was pulling out were slinky and provocative. Where were all the t-shirts? Her hoodies? The only pairs of jeans she found were her skinny jeans from the night before and a super tight flared leg.

"You're gonna look like a whore," the voice sang at her.

Samantha winced. It was true. She eventually fished out an off-the-shoulder crop top and the tight jeans. It wasn't a look she would have gone for normally, but given the options, seemed to be the only choice.

After getting dressed, she looked in the mirror and nearly cried. Her hair was a halo of frizz around her head, and she still had streaks of mascara running down her face.

"Ew," the voice piped up, "didn't you shower last night? How did you manage to get that wrong?"

She scrubbed her face mercilessly, then set about doing her hair and makeup. The reedy voice continued to berate her, questioning every decision she made. Her eyeliner- too heavy. Her lipstick- too red. Her hair- a ponytail, too basic.

By the time she finished, she was a wreck, but Rob was counting on her. He had gone downstairs while she was getting ready, giving her space to do her morning routine. She dug out her own lanyard, festooned with chibi cats, and hung it around her neck. The passes covered her belly a bit, but the weight of them pulled the lanyard into her cleavage. Her face reddened, and she tried adjusting her shirt to no avail. It was cut so that pulling it up made her belly hang out, but pulling it down made her chest hang out. She hated it. She looked down at her nails. She hated those too, unpainted and damaged from the nail glue. She looked in the mirror and came to the conclusion she came to most mornings.

She hated herself.

She smoothed her ponytail back one more time, grabbed her own backpack, then trudged downstairs. Rob stood by the door like an eager golden retriever. He smiled at her.

"You look great!" he exclaimed.

"Lies," the voice hissed.

"Thank you," Samantha said.

Rob opened the door and motioned her through. They piled into their car and made their way into the city. Samantha was quiet while Rob practiced his channel spiel. He planned on visiting all the important booths today to give out his card and present himself. Samantha planned on being his shadow and staying invisible as much as possible.

They parked in a pay lot, then started walking through the city. When they reached the cafe, the line snaked out the door.

"Yeah, I don't know about this," Rob said, squinting at the line.

"Rob! Samantha!" a voice called out from behind them.

They turned to see Todd and Jason bounding towards them.

"Change of plans," Todd said. "Cameron and Sarah are skipping breakfast to try to get in early."

"But," Jason interjected, "some of the guys found a place down the block and have a huge table reserved. Did you want to join them instead?"

Rob looked at Samantha. "What do you think?" he asked.

Samantha thought for a moment and shrugged. "Sure, sounds good."

Todd and Rob high-fived.

"Sweet!" Todd exclaimed. "Let's go get some food!"

He grabbed Jason's arm and started to drag him down the street. Rob slung an arm around Samantha's shoulders and followed them. As they walked into the restaurant, a huge booming cry rang out.

"ROBKET!"

Rob grinned sheepishly and took a bow. The table full of middle aged men began to applaud wildly. He walked over and started handing out business cards to many oohs and aahs. Samantha smiled awkwardly, hanging back a moment.

"You don't belong here," the voice whispered. "They don't care about you."

Jason walked over and grabbed Samantha's hand, pulling her over to their corner of the table. Todd nodded at her and passed her a menu. Aware of her belly spilling over the edge of her jeans, she glanced at it and decided a black coffee would suffice.

She had nearly finished her first cup before Rob sat down next to her. The conversation had turned to what booths were going to be at the convention, and who was planning to show up. They excitedly began to talk about one streamer in particular, who had started to delve into the art scene online.

"Ooh," Todd piped up, "That's what Sam's wanting to do! She's going to be starting up an art stream."

Samantha choked on her coffee. Suddenly, all eyes were on her.

"Is that so?" one guy asked, peering at her over thick lenses and a bushy beard.

"Um, yeah," she slowly said. "I mean, once the convention is over, sure."

"You'd be really good at it," another man, thin with a shock of red hair, said. "You've got the personality for it, for sure!"

"Yeah," the first guy said. "We've seen you in Rob's posts. We think you're great!"

A warm wave flowed over her. She didn't know these guys, and they were being so nice!

"Wait for it," the voice said sneeringly.

"You're like one of those girls," another man said, flipping his blonde hair back, "who doesn't act like a girl, you know? You're like a guy, really."

"Oooh, yeah," Jason said. "You're nothing like those cam girls."

"Like that kitten chick!" one of them chimed in.

"There it is," the voice finished, with an audible grin.

Samantha weakly smiled at him. The rest of the table murmured in agreement.

"Did you see the stream where she was wearing the blue fishnets? I never thought they'd allow her to broadcast herself wearing that one piece," said another.

"She knows what she wants, what she likes, and how to get it," the bearded man chuckled.

Samantha's face grew hot. She felt like her periphery was pulling and stretching in unnatural directions. Her eyes tunneled to her coffee, and she began to chew on the inside of her cheek. It was always Cassie.

"You've done a few streams with her, right, Rob?" Todd asked.

"Oh yeah," he replied, "I always have a great time. She's got wonderful energy, and she will shoot your ship down in a heartbeat, no warning whatsoever. She games harder than I do!"

The table roared with laughter, except for Samantha who was still staring at her drink. She felt a kick underneath the table and looked up to see Jason looking at her with concern. He raised his eyebrow quizzically and gave her a thumbs up. She tightened her lips into a curt smile and nodded. That seemed to be all he needed, and he dove back into the conversation.

The voice started to run through her head again. Every unsexy thing she had ever done or said, every awkward moment, every misunderstanding began to play out in her brain. She was ugly, she was clumsy, she was gross, she was fat. Her stomach growled, and Samantha shot it an angry glare. How dare it speak up in a moment like this. Did it not have enough flesh layered on top of it?

The rest of the breakfast rushed by in blur, like Samantha was watching it pass by a car window. She watched herself walk out and down the street towards the convention center. They stood in line, and she felt herself floating in the words around her. Her vision was blurry, and her senses were numb. She barely noticed them going through security. She barely felt it when Sarah wrapped her up in a big hug once they were inside.

She followed Rob in a daze as he wheeled and dealed. Cards were passed back and forth; he started a small collection in the front pocket of his backpack, asking Samantha to place each new one in there. She obliged, silent and mechanical.

At one point, they ended up at a colorful merch booth, and she felt herself shift back into her body. As she wrapped her fingers around the wooly socks and cold metal pins, her senses returned. She caught a whiff of popcorn coming from the next table down, and her stomach growled again. They bought a couple of t-shirts, much to Samantha's relief, and a plush creature from one of her favorite games. She then grabbed Rob's elbow and pulled him to the next table where he bought her a giant bag of buttered popcorn.

She happily shoved a handful of popcorn in her mouth. Rob laughed and brushed a piece off her chin.

"You seem like you're in a better mood," he said.

Samantha nodded and pointed at the popcorn. He laughed again.

"I can always count on food with you," he teased.

Samantha closed her eyes and happily wiggled her hips. When she opened her eyes, though, she saw her.

Standing in a ripped, low cut t-shirt and tiny cut off shorts, with a mess of cherry red hair curling around her face, was Cassie. She was taking a picture with a couple of fans, kicking her foot back and blowing a kiss to the camera. They hugged her and walked off, and Cassie turned and made eye contact with Samantha. Her eyes grew wide, and she started to stalk towards them.

Samantha grabbed Rob's hand and tugged. "Let's go check this booth out," she said, pulling at him desperately.

Rob looked at her, puzzled. "No, you should finish your popcorn first. You don't want it to go stale."

Samantha tugged at him again. "No, really, it's fine, let's go look at the-"

It was too late. The screech rang out from ten feet away.

"OH MY GOD, ROBKET?!"

Rob turned and flung his arms open.

"KITTY CAT CASSIE!"

They both ran towards each other, melding into a big hug. Cassie kicked her foot out again and bounced up and down. Rob held onto her shoulders and looked her up and down.

"I can't believe it! We're actually meeting in real life!"

She framed his face in her hands.
"Right?! You're real! And you're right in front of me!"

Samantha turned on her heel, threw her popcorn in the nearest trash can, and disappeared into the crowd. She pushed past people, squeezing through crowds of cosplayers and darting around booth workers. She wasn't sure where she was going, but she was determined to get there quickly.

She eventually flung herself out of the throng and threw herself at the concrete wall. She spun around and scanned the people in front of her, looking for familiar faces. Finding none, she retreated to the restrooms.

An elf was bent over the sink, touching up her makeup. She flicked her eyes in Samantha's direction. Samantha gave her an awkward smile and ducked into a stall. She threw her backpack up on the door hook, then sat down on the toilet. Her breathing was shallow and rapid, and the stall swam around her.

She shakily pulled her phone out and glanced at it. There was no signal, not that Rob would have noticed her absence by then, she figured. She scrolled back and forth across the screens aimlessly.

"Deep breaths," a calm voice murmured.

Samantha took the advice and closed her eyes while she breathed. Slowly, the panic was replaced with steadiness, and she could think clearly again. She didn't have any signal and needed to find Rob again. If Cassie was still with him, she wasn't sure what she would do, but she couldn't be left stranded at the convention on her own.

She heard the bathroom door swing open and shut and figured the elf had left. She gathered herself together, swung her backpack over her shoulder, and strode out. To her surprise, the elf was still there. Samantha quietly sidled up to the sinks and began to wash her hands.

"Sweetie, are you doing alright?"

Samantha turned to see the other woman staring at her quizzically.

"Oh, uh, yeah, I'm fine," she stammered, "just a lot of people out there you know?"

The elf with the southern twang nodded reassuringly.

"If you need it," she said, "there's a quiet room upstairs, just down the hall from the panel rooms. They've got coloring pages, comic books, and some beanbag chairs. I know it's helped me out in the past."

A warm wave swept through Samantha's chest.

"Thank you," she replied sincerely. "I will check it out."

The elf smiled at her and turned back to her makeup. Samantha wasn't sure what compelled the woman to be so nice, but it had made her day.

"Women have to look out for each other," the calm voice said.

Samantha agreed and immediately felt ashamed by her frantic fleeing moments before. There was no need to react the way she had. She had her moment alone to reconvene with herself, and now she would need to find Rob again.

She dried her hands and snuck another glance at the elf. The woman caught her and gave her two thumbs up.

"You've got this, darling! Have a good con!"

Samantha smiled and waved goodbye. There would always be something magical about supportive women in the restroom.

As she stepped back into the bustle of the crowd, she took another deep breath and glanced around. There were still no familiar faces. She drifted around, table to table, darting her head to and fro. She found herself back where she had run away but found no Rob.

Panic began to set in again. She walked a straight line until she got to the edge of the room once more and began to circle around. In the sea of faces, she recognized not a one. Suddenly the lights were too bright and the sounds were too loud. She found an escalator and clung to the railing. Once she reached the top, she ran to the edge and scanned the crowd from above. She tried looking for Cassie's red hair to see if she was still with Rob, but there were far too many people with the same shade to tell.

She wandered into the lobby and felt her pocket vibrate. She looked down and saw a bevy of texts had come through. She scrolled through them.

"Where'd you go?"

"Where are you?"

"I'll be in the lobby next to the statue."

"Where are you?"

"Jason said he saw you head to the bathroom. Are you okay?"

"Where are you?"

"I'm going to the influencer panel. Meet me outside after."

She put the phone away and walked over to a map. Next to it were schedules of the various panels and shows. It looked like

Rob's panel was going to be over in half an hour. She would have time to look around some of the art booths at that point.

She smiled at the idea of picking up some space art for Rob and maybe some sketchbooks for herself. She turned around and nearly ran face first into someone. As she was about to push out a "sorry", she looked up.

It was Cassie.

She smirked at Samantha.

"Wow, I almost didn't recognize you. You're looking a lot healthier these days."

Samantha looked down to see that her belly was pushing out under her crop top, accentuating the fupa her tight jeans had manifested.

"I'm sorry, do I know you?"

The words tumbled out of Samantha's mouth so fast, she couldn't remember even thinking them. It was as if something else had taken over.

Cassie raised an eyebrow.

"Yeah, Kitty Cat Cassie. I play games with Robket. I guess we've never actually met, but I figured you would remember me jumping on his stream."

"Oh," Samantha found herself saying, "now I'm remembering. You're the one who does the pvp games? All the war stuff?"

Cassie's head tilted.

"No, that's Awol Lola. Or Camola. I do more rp than anything."

Samantha shook her head and shrugged. "Sorry. You all just seem so similar. Guess it's just a cam girl thing."

Cassie looked taken aback. Samantha turned on her heel and walked away towards the art booths.

What was that, she wondered. It definitely hadn't been her speaking. If not her, then who?

She wandered around the booths in a daze. It wasn't until Rob grabbed her arm did she come to. She found herself holding a notebook with panties printed on the outside. Not her usual style, but it was cute enough.

"I thought we were going to meet outside the panel room," he said. "Did you get my message?"

"I did," Samantha replied. "I just lost track of time. Speaking of, what time is it?"

"It's been over an hour," Rob replied.

"Oh shit!" Samantha exclaimed. "I'm sorry. I didn't even know."

Rob waved a hand. "It's fine," he said. "I met up with some people on the panel and talked some shop with them. They pointed me in a few good directions, so I've got a few more booths to hit up. After that, want to go back to the house and get ready for a bar meet up?"

Samantha smiled at him. "Of course. That sounds great! Will you put this book away before we go?"

Rob took it from her and zipped it up. It sounded like he struggled with it, but a moment later, he patted her on the head, took her hand, and led her through the crowd. They visited a start-up that linked all social media on one dashboard. They promised Rob he could easily increase his presence while posting big announcements on multiple platforms with one command. He seemed very interested and exchanged information with them for later.

Samantha took interest in it as she was always trying to minimize and organize and thought it would be a great way to keep track of everything. The next booth, dedicated to a popular tabletop war game, was less interesting to her. She knew Rob had been dying to get a partnership with them, though, so she stuck by him. She danced to and fro in the background. Standing on concrete all day had done a number on her feet and legs.

The final booth they visited for the day was a military charity. At this point, her feet were on fire. Somehow, the head guy at the booth stood motionless in a pair of big heavy boots. Samantha was in utter awe at him. Rob was never in the military, but Samantha's father was. Rob always joked that he needed to make up for the fact that he was dating and engaged to a military man's only daughter, to try to stay on his good side. Given her father's temper, Samantha was inclined to encourage him.

The charity was an absolute success. Rob loved the program, and the people there were aware of his channel. They agreed to work together on some fundraising events and made a note to meet up again before the convention was over.

As they went to leave, they ran into Cameron and Sarah.

"How's the con going?" Sarah asked. "Get some good stuff?"

"You know it," Rob answered, patting Samantha's backpack. It was rather heavy.

Cameron pointed at Rob. "Hang out after the bar?"

Rob pointed back. "Hang out after the bar!"

Sarah gave Samantha a quick hug. "We have to go find Paige and Josh, but we'll meet up with you there!"

Paige and Josh were a streamer couple that Rob was friends with. Samantha suspected they would bump into each other at some point.

They left the convention center and headed back to the car. On the way there, Rob gave Samantha a concerned look.

"Are you feeling okay?" he asked.

"Yeah, absolutely," Samantha replied. "Just tired. A little headachey, too."

She wasn't lying. Ever since they left the art booths, her head had been in splitting pain.

"Well, you haven't really eaten anything. Maybe we should get some real food before we get to the bar?"

"Nah," she replied, "I'll be fine. I can grab something there. Something fried and carby."

Rob grinned. "That's my Sam."

They got into the car and headed back to the house. Exhausted, Samantha threw herself onto the couch. Rob tugged at her arm.

"Shower time, let's go."

"No," Samantha groaned. "Nap first, then shower."
"We have to be at the bar in two hours," Rob said, "and we need to get you food before that."

"I'll be fine," she said. "I'll eat food there. Just a quick nap."

Rob sighed. "Alright. Thirty minutes. That's all you get. I know it takes you a while to get ready."

Samantha couldn't respond to that one, because she was already asleep.

Chapter Nine

I found myself on the idyllic street again. This time, it was overcast and windy. The trees whipped around, scattering their Leaves down the sidewalk. Once again, the streets were empty and there were no people strolling along the sidewalk. The piano store was still there, but the cat had left the display. There was a chill in the air that managed to permeate my thick, grey sweater. I tugged my beanie down further over my ears and wriggled my nose happily. This was the kind of stormy fall weather I deeply enjoyed.

I walked over to one of the benches and perched on the end of it. I looked up to the sky and watched thick, dark rain clouds roll in. I didn't have an umbrella, but there were plenty of awnings if I needed shelter. A deep rumble rose up in the distance, and the wind howled wildly. Still, there was a sort of peace to everything, like the pause in a deep breath.

"You caused quite a stir earlier," a voice quipped beside me.

I turned to find Eric sitting next to me, kicked back with one leg balanced on his knee, his hands clasped behind his head.

"What do you mean?" I asked.

"What do I mean?" he retorted. "Charity, Ariana, storming the file room. Everyone was in shambles by the time you left."

I considered this for a moment. "I still don't know what any of this is," I replied.

"Nor should you," he replied, winking at me.

"If it involves me, then I feel I should," I flung back.

He raised his hands in a classic "don't shoot the messenger" manner.

"All I'm saying is this is the kind of stuff you figure out for yourself," he calmly replied. "I admit, Thomas could be a little more forthcoming and a little less man of mystery, but the fact remains that we only know so much ourselves."

"Well, what do you know?" I probed.

He grinned. "Now now, you don't help a baby chick peck it's way out of the shell. What do you think we know?"

I paused. He nodded and turned his attention to some leaves skittering down the street.

"I think you know more about the panic eyes than you let on," I finally said. "I think there is something about the mouse, and I think you are all keeping secrets from me."

He looked over at me and seemed to ponder for a moment.

"I would counter," he said, "that we only know as much about the panic eyes as you do. As for the mouse, it's a bit like these clouds. You know there's a storm on the way."

He leaned over closer to me.

"And we all have secrets, darling," he whispered conspiratorially.

"What's one of yours?" I whispered back, mocking his tone.

His grin spread even wider. "I'm very fond of pineapple."

I groaned and stood up.

"I'm not going to get any information out of you, am I?" I asked.

"Oh, sweetie, I'm not here for that," he replied.

"Well, then why are you here?"

He patted the space on the bench next to him. I shook my head. He sighed and stood up.

"I'm here to make sure you're okay. You seem to be having a tough time of it, and I want to be here for you."

"I'm fine," I said sharply.

"That's why you hid in the bathroom?"

I blinked at him.

"How do you know about that?"

He tapped the side of my head gently. "Didn't you say I live in there? If I did, then surely I would know what you're going through."

"You never said you did, though," I replied.

"I never said I didn't," he smirked.

We stared at each other for a long beat. That feeling of familiarity washed over me again.

"Why do I feel like I've known you forever?" I asked.

"Maybe you have," he answered with a small smile.

"And the others?"

He shrugged. "More or less. You can't say their voices are unfamiliar."

He was right. I did listen to them day in and day out.

Suddenly, a loud boom of thunder rang out, and I jumped.

"Eric, what are you doing?"

I turned to see Ariana walking up to us, her curls bouncing with each step. She seemed like she was on a mission, and Eric was the target.

"Just enjoying this lovely day, miss. Thought we'd soak up some rays and show our appreciation for the great outdoors," he replied with his trademark grin.

Ariana stood next to him, glaring up at him with a disapproving purse to her lips. She barely came up to his chest.

"You can't be out here if it starts to rain; you'll get her sick," she said.

He tilted his head. "Key word is if, and you know it."

She rolled her eyes and looked at me.

"How are you doing? Are you holding up okay?"

I nodded quietly.

She nodded back. "I'm sorry for earlier. I wanted to make sure you were safe, and I may have gotten carried away."

I squinted a little. There was something about seeing the two of them standing together that bristled in my mind more than her halfhearted apology.

"Have you . . . always kept me safe?" I asked.

Her eyes grew wide, and her head snapped towards Eric.

"What have you told her?" she demanded.

"Nothing she didn't already know," he cooly replied.

"No," she said, pointing a finger at him. "Don't you dare be flippant with me. What did you tell her?"

"I think that's between me and her," he replied, nodding his head towards me.

Ariana's face flushed, and she looked at me, lips pulled tight.

"Whatever he said, you don't need to worry about it. I have everything under control."

I raised my hands. "Sure you do. It's cool."

She shook her head. "I'm being serious. With everything going on outside, you don't need to worry about what's going on in here."

I furrowed my eyebrows. "In here?"

Ariana's eyes widened again. She frantically looked at Eric. He smiled widely.

"Told you I didn't tell her anything she didn't know."

The thunder began to rumble again, and rain started to fall. Eric looked genuinely shocked.

"Well, I'll be," he mumbled.

Ariana grabbed my arm and pulled me underneath an awning.

"What did you mean, in here?" I asked again.

The rain came down harder, and Eric loped over to huddle up with us. In the distance, I could hear a faint noise growing louder.

"I meant . . . in your dreams, is what I meant," she said, with a catch in her voice. "Speaking of you should wake up now."

"I don't think that's what you meant," I replied, "and why are you always trying to wake me up?"

"It's not healthy for you to be here like this," she shouted over the thunder and rain.

"Like what?" I asked. The sound grew louder; I could almost make it out.

She gestured around herself. "Out in a storm. Out in the open."

"Outside?" I added.

She pointed her finger at me this time and tilted her head.

"Don't. Don't get smart."

The sound burst forward as a bolt of lightning flashed in the sky. It was someone crying. Their wails echoed around the buildings and shook the trees. They seemed to cause the storm to swell, as the rain and thunder began to pick up. Everything was dark grey, and the rain was starting to rush sideways. Ariana moved to shield me while Eric rubbed his arms.

"We really should get out of this," he said, giving the storm a leery look.

"As I was saying before," Ariana replied with a cool stare.

"Where's that man when you need him?" Eric asked, ignoring her.

I looked around, but I could barely see a few feet in front of me. The crying had grown louder, and the thunder shook the ground.

"There he is!" Eric cried out and pointed his finger.

I followed his gesture to the corner of the street. At first, I couldn't see anything, but then a large flash of lightning lit up the block. A giant umbrella the size of a merry-go-round was illuminated for a moment. It was blue, with small yellow daisies dancing across it. A pair of long, thin legs strode underneath it.

With each burst of lightning, the umbrella drew nearer. Eventually, the edge came right up to our awning and tilted up. Underneath was the thin, dark haired man from the file room, the one I assumed to be Thomas. He looked unamused as usual.

"Everyone, get underneath," he called out, motioning with one hand for us to join him.

Ariana grabbed my hand and we darted over to him, with Eric closely following. Once we were under the umbrella, he gave it a twirl, letting the edge dance along the sidewalk. The storm and the crying quieted, and when he tilted it back up, we were standing in the room with the piano. He closed the umbrella and set it aside.

Eric looked around, seemingly unimpressed with his surroundings. Ariana, on the other hand, stared at her feet. Thomas turned and took a deep breath.

"How did you come to be in the storm?"

"I told her to wake up," Ariana replied quietly.

"And you didn't?" he asked me.

I shook my head, suddenly nervous as thought caught doing something bad.

"Why not?" he probed.

"I was talking to Eric," I said. "I didn't think it was actually going to storm."

"Eric?" he asked, raising an eyebrow.

Eric shrugged. "What she said. We were having a lovely conversation, and then, boom, sudden storm."

Thomas shook his head. "You should know better," he said.

He sat down at the piano, plucked at a few keys, then stared thoughtfully at them.

"This has gotten too far out of hand," he mumbled.

Ariana looked up.

"It was me," she said. "If I hadn't gone after Charity like I had, then none of this would have happened."

Thomas raised a hand. "No, no. That's not it. We can fix this."

He spun around in his seat and looked at me.

"I am so very sorry for all of this. You should not have been exposed to any of it."

"To what?" I asked, very confused.
"You aren't ready," he continued. "While the panic eyes run rampant, we can't expect you to shoulder anything else."

"Like what?" I asked again.

"Eric, can you fetch me my tools?"

Eric furrowed his brow. "Really, Tom? That's how we're going to play it?"

"Play what?" I asked frantically.

Ariana placed a hand on my shoulder.

"You're okay," she said. "Thomas knows what he's doing."

Eric walked out of the room, into the file room. A moment later he emerged with a hammer and a brush. He hesitated a moment, then begrudgingly handed them over.

"I just don't think it's right," he said.

"It's what we have to do," Thomas said. He stood up and approached me.

I instinctively tried to run, but I found myself frozen to the spot, my legs tensing up in futility. Ariana's grip on my shoulder deepened.

Thomas shifted the brush and hammer to his right hand and raised his left. He set it on top of my head, then let his fingers drip down my face, sliding my eyelids shut.

Chapter Ten

Samantha woke up to a blinding headache. She could feel her scalp tightening and the muscles behind her eyes pulsating. She checked the time on her phone and was shocked to see an hour had passed. She felt like she had just closed her eyes. She groaned and ran her fingers through her hair.

"You awake?" Rob asked gently from across the room.

Samantha looked up at him. He was sprawled out in an armchair, tapping away at his phone.

"I think so," she grimaced.

"Sounded like you were having a bad one," he said, casually scrolling a finger across the screen.

"Then why didn't you wake me up?" she asked.

He shrugged. "The last time I tried to wake you up from a nightmare, you tried to launch your knee into my nuts. Not making that mistake again."

Samantha nodded begrudgingly and stood up. Her knees shook, and she fell back onto the sofa. Rob dropped his phone onto the side table and ran over.

"Are you okay?" he asked, reaching out to steady her.

"Yeah," she answered, "just stood up too fast."

In all honesty, it felt like her brain had smashed against her skull. The pressure in her head was overwhelming.

She staggered into the kitchen and poured a glass of water. As she sipped it, her thoughts began to swirl.

"Drink it slowly, not too fast."

"Shouldn't have taken that nap."

"Stood up too fast? Shouldn't have stood up at all!"

"Exactly! Go lie down again."

"Got to get ready for the bar. What are you going to wear?"

"Who's going to even want you there? You're just going to bring the whole vibe down."

"Yeah, you should just stay here and wallow in it."

"Or take a bath. That could help the headache, too!"

Rob dutifully walked over and handed her some ibuprofen. She thanked him and swallowed the pills as quickly as she could.

"Are you going to be good to go out tonight?" he asked.

"NO!" came the resounding cry in her head, multiple voices entwining into one.

"Yeah, I should be fine," she said.

She set the glass in the sink and started to make her way to the bedroom, carefully taking one step at time, wincing with each movement.

"What is the vibe going to be?" she asked. "Casual, dressy?"

"Oh, casual for sure," Rob replied. "Jeans and tshirt kind of event."

That was a relief to Samantha. She could at least be comfortable while they were there. She hoisted her backpack up onto the bed, unzipping it so she could retrieve a tshirt.

She reached in and pulled out the notebook she had been holding when Rob found her. She flipped through it a bit, admiring the different watercolor prints on each of the pages. She set it aside with a smile and reached in again. Her hand grabbed something soft. She immediately thought of the plushie they had bought before the whole scene with Cassie went down. When she pulled it out, however, she was shocked to see that it was an entirely different stuffed animal. She turned the small fairy around in her hands, examining it closely for any spark of recognition. When there was none, she assumed it had been a sneaky gift from Rob and placed it on the bed. She then took out a set of cat ears, also unfamiliar, but guessed that they had come with one of the other items. She removed stacks of brochures and maps, the original plushie she had bought, and, finally, her tshirts. She decided on the one with a rainbow prism exploding into a bunch of dice. It was cute enough, a little black tee, but still casual.

She undressed, setting her jeans with the shirt, and hopped into the shower. As the steam hit her, she felt her headache start to subside. Maybe the bar event wouldn't be so bad after all.

She kept her hair away from the water, so when she stepped out, it was simple enough to pile it into a messy bun on top of her head. She decided to go a little heavy with the eye makeup, partially to complement the black shirt, partially because she was having trouble keeping her hands steady.

Samantha looked herself over in the mirror, decided it would work, and headed back downstairs. Rob must have heard her, because he was digging his feet into his shoes and tossing his keys and wallet into his shorts pocket. He, as usual, was going in costume.

"I feel underdressed with you in that vest and tie," she teased.

"Then just focus on the waist down," he said with a wink.

She slapped his arm playfully and rolled her eyes.

"Oh, Rob," a voice chimed in. "This is why we love ya."

Samantha smiled. The headache was just barely there, and there was enough fun going around that she was hopeful for how the rest of the night would turn out.

Knowing they were going to have some drinks, Rob got them a ride share. They hopped into the unfamiliar car and greeted the driver.

She was a nice older woman who let them know that the bar they were going to used to be a speakeasy back in the day. She regaled them with tales of the city, where to get the best breakfast that next morning, what museums they may want to check out while they were there, the top spots for live music that weekend. In return, they eagerly filled her in on what was happening with the convention, just how many different places and people were being represented there, and how much they had enjoyed the trip so far.

When they arrived, they left with many waves and thanks, having made a new friend, no matter how temporarily. Rob placed a hand on the small of Samantha's back and led her over to the bar. A bouncer just inside the door checked their ids and directed them to the rooftop where everyone else would be. Samantha noticed on their way in that many of the women there were wearing club attire, short dresses, tight tops, glitz and glam everywhere. They were all gathered at the bar downstairs, though, so she shook the thoughts off.

Not now, she thought to herself, directing the voices to leave her alone.

They climbed the stairs, passing other people as they went. Again, Samantha noticed that, while the men were wearing t-shirts or casual button downs, the women were all dressed up. She started to get nervous.

They finally made it four flights up to the rooftop. As Samantha scanned the crowd, her worst fears came true. Gorgeously styled hair, skin-tight slinky dresses, stilettos, freshly manicured nails, and expertly applied makeup flashed their perfection in front of her. She scuffed her sneakers together and tugged at the bottom of her shirt. She was far underdressed.

"Go home, go home now," a voice chimed in.

"It's not too late. Maybe that nice lady is still nearby; check your app!"

"How dare Rob do this to you. He knew!"

"How dare Rob? You should have been willing to dress up in the first place!"

"Just have a few drinks, you'll be fine."

"That's a great idea! Maybe a pina colada! That would be refreshing."

"Rob and Sam! Over here!!"

They turned to see Paige and Josh waving them over to a large table with a wraparound couch. Cameron sat next to them, his arm slung around Sarah. They were laughing with another couple that Samantha didn't recognize. Four guys sat next to them, engrossed in their own conversation. Paige stood up and lifted her drink up at them, continuing to wave. She was already tall but was sporting a staggering set of heels and a tiny black cocktail dress. As they got closer, Samantha could see that even Sarah, who usually wore big comfy sweaters and yoga pants, was wearing a ruffled metallic dress.

She grabbed Rob's arm and hissed in his ear, "I thought you said this was casual."

He shrugged. "I thought it was. It's just a bar and some drinks with friends. I didn't think everyone would dress up."

Her grip on his arm tightened. "I can't be here like this."

"You'll be fine," he said, patting her hand. "We'll get some drinks and relax. It'll be okay; you'll see."

He gave her a big smile and a kiss on the cheek.

This didn't settle her nerves. Her headache started to flare up again.

When they arrived at the table, Paige ran over and hugged them.

"It's so good to see you, Rob! And Sam, you look amazing as always! You weren't feeling the crop top from earlier?"

Samantha tilted her head. She didn't recall seeing Paige.

"Uh, no. I decided to go with something a little more casual."

Paige smiled. "You are always so true to yourself. I think it's great that you are comfortable in your own skin."

Samantha blushed. She was not comfortable at all.

Rob patted her on the back. "Where can we get food and drinks?" he yelled over the crowd.

Paige gestured around the room. "There's a waitress who comes around every few minutes. I think Theo has the menu."

Rob nodded. "Good deal. Someone hasn't eaten yet." He poked Samantha's ribs.

Paige slapped Samantha on the arm. "Why didn't you tell me? Josh and I would've invited you to grab some food with us."

Samantha frowned in confusion. "Grab some food?"

Paige nodded enthusiastically. "Yeah. That's where we went after we hung out at the art booths. We took off because we were getting hungry."

Samantha was still confused. She didn't remember seeing Paige or Josh at all that day.

Rob tugged at her until she sat down next to him on the couch. He grabbed the attention of one of the guys, a slender man with green hair, and got him to pass a menu to them.

Feeling more embarrassed than hungry, Samantha decided to get some mozzarella sticks and a large pineapple margarita.

Soon after making this decision, the waitress did stop by the table. Rob opened a tab with her and ordered Samantha's picks, along with a beer for himself. He then turned towards the men he was sitting next to and began to shmooze.

Samantha couldn't help but be in awe. He was always so confident and outgoing. People naturally flocked to him. She could tell they were talking about streaming as she watched his whole face light up. He was in his element.

She wrapped her arms around herself. She was not.

Her food and drink arrived, and she stared at the plate while she ate. Over time, a group of women came over to the table and began to talk with Paige. They spotted Rob and pointed, talking quickly amongst themselves. Rob saw them and waved. They smiled and waved back. One girl walked over and leaned across Samantha like she wasn't there.

"I love your series on the different spaceships," she slurred. "It just makes the game so much more real, you know?"

Rob nodded. "Thank you! It means a lot!"

She placed a hand on his shoulder. "What are you going to do next?"

They started a conversation about his streaming plans while Samantha, huddled over the table, slowly fed herself cheese sticks and drained her margarita. The waitress must have spotted this, because as she took the last sip, she was there by the table, motioning if she wanted more. Samantha nodded emphatically and made a motion in return to keep the drinks coming.

By this time, the girls had moved over to where Rob and Samantha were and were talking animatedly with Rob. Business cards were flowing back and forth, and plans were made to do joint streams.

Samantha buried herself in her second drink. A moment later, she felt a tap on her shoulder. She looked up to see a beautiful blonde woman in a glittery white top staring down at her.

"I love your shirt!" she yelled over the noise.

Samantha gave her a little nod. "Thank you."

"I wanted to get one, but they were out of my size!"

Samantha nodded again.

"It's super hard being extra small sometimes, especially at events like this, you know?"

Samantha continued to nod but drained half of her margarita as she did.

"And finding something with print that goes over the boobs and not across or under them? Golden!"

Samantha set down her cheese stick and awkwardly swirled the drink in her glass. Her head was starting to feel a little fuzzy.

"Anyway, love the shirt!" the girl said again, before waltzing away.

Samantha finished her drink and signaled the waitress, who brought her another margarita, albeit with a bit of a side eye.

Over the next few minutes, Samantha fell into a blur of drinking, ordering more cheese sticks, and people watching. The voices in the room were loud enough to nearly drown out the ones inside. She started to relax and found herself talking to the people around her. She wasn't keeping up with the conversation or what she was consuming. It was like someone else was doing it for her. She sprawled out in her seat, settling her body weight in between her legs which she spread out wide in front of her. In no time, the whole table was turned towards her as she lit up into some story about a video game she had played. In the back of her mind, she commented on how impressed she was. It had only taken a few drinks to turn her into a social butterfly. She decided to kick back and let whatever was happening happen.

She thought about when she was younger, how her friends always teased her.

"You never talk to people," Rachel said, "But you never shut up with us!"

"She's just shy, is all," Jen replied. "You're comfortable with us, right?"

She was right. Everyone else was mean. They bullied her and made her feel awkward and unwanted. Rachel and Jen were always there to pick her back up, though. They were inseparable all throughout elementary, then middle and high schools. It was only after graduation that they fell out of touch and moved on to separate lives. Jen got married and had a bunch of kids. Rachel ran off to the west coast to figure herself out. Samantha met Rob and settled into banking. They were going to get married in the next few years, but they weren't in a rush about it.

The last time they had all spoken, both Jen and Rachel seemed extraordinarily happy with how their lives had turned out. Samantha was less so but put on a happy mask anyway. She didn't know how else things could have played out, but she felt like they could be better. She could have a job she enjoyed, she could be really good at a hobby, something could be in place that fulfilled her. Instead, she felt empty, like a hollow doll with a suitcase full of masks.

Samantha remembered that Rachel used to get upset with her. They would be playing or talking, and something would come up that would hurt Samantha. Some time later, she would be listening to Rachel chastise her over her mood swings and how she would seem like a different person. Samantha would apologize and change the subject. It was something else that made her "not normal", and she couldn't risk her friends leaving her because of it.

Samantha spent a lot of time with Rachel in particular. She would find out later that Rachel's life wasn't always sunshine and rainbows, either, but she would always remember those times fondly. There was never any shouting, nobody hit each other, and she never felt like she was being judged, except for the mood swings. They would stay up to three in the morning, telling stories and playing games, then wake up early to spend time with Rachel's grandmother.

When Rachel would fill her in later about the stress she had at home, Samantha was in shock. Jen had confirmed her own stresses, too, and it made Samantha feel less alone. Everyone had problems at home; she was normal! Well, almost.

The voices had developed right alongside her. They got to a point once where she would talk back to them to quiet them. She got caught doing that in school one day, and a mean girl in class, Elise, had decided to use that as ammo for the next several years. Elise was wealthier, always on the cheerleading squad, and never went to school without a full face of makeup. She made those years a living hell for Samantha. After graduation, whenever Samantha would see her in their small town, she would make a point of not talking to her. Thirteen years was already far too many to have to deal with Elise.

"What do you think, Sam?"

Samantha shook her head. She was sitting outside on a dock. Sarah was sitting next to her with a smile on her face. Cameron and Rob were off to the side, deeply engaged in conversation.

"Sure," she said cautiously.

Sarah clapped her hands and stood up.

"Boys, Sam and I want pancakes! Hurry up!"

They gave her a thumbs up and started to wrap up.

Samantha stood up and stretched. Her joints popped and her muscles screamed at her. She must have been sitting for quite some time. How many margaritas had she had? She felt sober now, but it must have been more than a few.

"I read about this little local place that's really close to our hotel. Did you want to check it out?"

Samantha nodded. "That sounds good."

Sarah gave her a concerned look. "We need to get you hydrated," she said. "Your voice is starting to change."

Samantha cleared her throat. "Yeah, I could use some water."

Sarah beamed at her. "You were quite the chatterbox tonight! It was nice seeing you so comfortable with everyone."

Samantha gave her a little smile. "Thank you."

Sarah nodded. "I think your stream is going to be a huge success!"

Oh no, Samantha thought. Not that again.

As the guys ordered up a car, she began to panic. She didn't have enough time or energy to stream. Even so, what would she do? She sucked at art, she sucked at video games, and she definitely wasn't going to bare it all for the camera.

"It'll be fun!" a laid back voice said. "Something for you to look forward to each day at work!"

"The only way to not suck at something is to do it," another voice lectured. "If you're doing it everyday, especially in front of an audience, you're going to get better at it."

"Or you'll be a complete failure," yet another one chimed in, "so why even bother?"

The car arrived, and they all got in. The driver, a younger man, started to chat with them. Rob, Cameron, and Sarah chipperly joined in, but Samantha stared out the window. Her mind was reeling, and her head was pulsing. She didn't really want to go out for food. She wanted to go back to their place and curl up in bed.

They piled into a booth at the diner, and Samantha still looked out the window. Cars flew by on the road outside, but inside, the pace was slow and methodical. A few older people dotted the restaurant, and a tired looking couple with a young, wide awake child sat in a back booth. A few people with convention passes walked past outside.

"Here ya go," Rob said, handing her a menu.

Samantha skimmed it. As she looked over the pictures, her stomach rumbled. It seemed like she needed pancakes after all.

The waiter came by and took their orders. Samantha's was the simplest: pancake, scrambled egg, and sausage with a glass of orange juice. Everyone else was getting whipped cream and other toppings, but she just wanted plain carbs.

Rob drank his coffee with one hand and rubbed Samantha's knee with the other. He shot her concerned looks every so often. She tapped the side of her head to indicate a headache, and he nodded. Her feet were still throbbing, too. She wasn't sure how she was going to make it through two and half more days of convention. When they got their food, she found herself downing it like she hadn't eaten in days.

Note to self, she thought, food is necessary to get through this.

"So what are you guys going to do tomorrow?" Sarah asked.

"Well," Rob said, "everyone else is supposed to show up tomorrow, so I'm going to be meeting up with people all day, then going to that soiree at night. We did our shopping already, but there are supposed to be some good panels. I think that's what Sam's going to be doing, right?"

Samantha nodded. "There are a few psychological ones I want to attend," she said. "Depression in Gaming, Can I Stream with Anxiety, Games and Anger Issues, those sorts of things."

Cameron laughed a little. "Not that whole 'video games make people violent' discourse?"

"That's what it sounds like," Samantha said. "I'm interested to see how the mental health people and industry experts address it."

"I think the anxiety one is interesting," Sarah chimed in. "They say streaming is like putting on a different persona. It would be fascinating to find out which personalities are actually struggling with those issues while putting on a brave face."

"It's more than you would think," Rob said. "I don't have too many issues with it, but I know others who have. Kitty Cat Cassie, for example."

Samantha's brain immediately turned to static.

"She has so many self image issues," he confessed.

"But she's so pretty!" Sarah gasped.

"They say it's harder for them," Cameron said solemnly. "When beauty is all the focus, it consumes you."

"What do you mean by them?" Sarah asked, raising an eyebrow.

Cameron rolled his eyes, "Don't start with me, woman."

Rob laughed. "It's her whole thing," he said, becoming serious again. "She has to look good all the time."

Sarah shook her head. "I would have never guessed."

Samantha stared at the table. The voices were swarming her again, telling her she wasn't pretty, reminding her of all the time Rob spent with Cassie, how everyone liked her more than Samantha. She felt sick to her stomach.

"Oh and CowRed, too," he said. "He's bipolar."

Cameron nodded. "He's done a few streams about that," he added.

Sarah's eyes widened. "Really?"

Samantha blinked and looked up. "Yeah," she said weakly. "He did a whole series for a mental health fundraiser event. He's bipolar one."

"Wow," Sarah said, "I wonder if that's why he does so many twenty-four hour streams?"

The bell on the door jingled, and a pack of people in purple hoodies walked in, sporting their convention passes on their bright orange lanyards. These were some sort of bigwigs, people who ran a booth or an organization. The booth got quiet as they walked past.

"Do you recognize any of them?" asked Cameron.

Rob shook his head. "No," he said. "The tall redhead looks familiar, but I'm not sure where I know him."

Sarah shoved Cameron. "Go talk to them," she said.

The guys faltered and started murmuring excuses.

"No, none of that, go introduce yourselves," she continued, while pushing Cameron out of the booth.

Both guys fumbled with their pockets, pulled out business cards, and walked over. Sarah and Samantha watched as they addressed the group, who immediately began shaking their hands and pulling them down to sit with them.

"Sometimes you just have to give someone a little push," Sarah said with a smile.

Samantha agreed and took a sip of her orange juice.

"So what do we have against Cassie?" Sarah asked.

Samantha choked a little.

"What do you mean?" she asked.

"Please, you get all clammed up whenever her name comes up. You called her an alcoholic whore at the bar tonight."

Samantha's eyes widened. "I did?"

Sarah laughed. "Well, to be honest, I didn't expect you to remember it. That was probably your fourth or fifth margarita."

Samantha blushed. She didn't mean for those thoughts to make their way out.

"All I'm saying," Sarah said, "is the last time I saw her around other people, she was passed out on a pool table, clutching an empty bottle of vodka."

Samantha's stomach sank. "No."

Sarah nodded. "Happened at a convention last year. Another girl and I had to wake her up and get her to her room. I agree, the girl has issues with alcohol, but what has she done to get you so hateful towards her?"

Samantha shook her head. "Nothing, I just, I don't know."

"Is it Rob?" Sarah asked. "I know they talk a lot, but you have the ring. She's not a threat. I've seen the way he looks at you. I don't think anyone could come between you two."

Samantha nodded. "Yeah, that's not it at all. We just don't mix, you know?"

Before Sarah could answer, the two men had returned, flipping through the business cards in their hands.

"They're game devs!" Rob cried out.

"They want us to test their game tomorrow morning, on stream!" Cameron added.

"Good!" Sarah said. "Aren't you glad you talked to them?"

They started bombarding her with details about the game. Samantha half-listened, thinking about the conversation she just had. Maybe she had been too harsh with Cassie after all. If Sarah wasn't worried about her, why was Samantha? Cassie talked to Cameron, too.

"Sarah's prettier than you," a voice reminded her. "Of course she's not threatened."

Samantha pushed past it. She was certain she had been mistaken, and she was determined now to make her convention a better one. She was going to go to her panels, maybe do a little more shopping, and enjoy her time there. Knowing that Cassie had such a vulnerable moment with Sarah made her more human and less intimidating. She was just another person; why should Samantha be so unsettled?

They finished their food and left the restaurant. There were hugs all around, and Rob ordered a car to take them home. Sarah and Cameron traipsed down the sidewalk towards their hotel, holding hands and chatting with each other.

"I like hanging out with them," Samantha declared.

"Me, too," Rob agreed. "They're cool people."

The older gentleman who picked them up was very quiet. They rode back to the house in silence, and Samantha started to drift off to sleep. She checked her phone to find it was three in the morning.

"Just like old times," a voice said wistfully.

She nodded quietly. The car stopped, and Rob helped her get out.

"I think we'll sleep in," he said with a comforting tone.

Samantha yawned. "That would be lovely."

They went upstairs and curled up in bed, Rob snoring just seconds before Samantha fell asleep.

Chapter Eleven

I was in the top room of the tower, sitting at the piano. Pages of sheet music were scattered all around me. I brushed my fingers lightly against the keys, feeling the cool, worn ivory against my fingertips. I plucked one and listened to it reverberate against the walls. I turned to look around.

There was a large, open window behind me, with stacks of paper and books strewn about haphazardly. It was cloudy outside, and the sky was grey. There was a plain wall next to it, with a fireplace around the corner from that. There was no fire, but there were ashes in the bottom, swirling about with each breeze that came in. The final wall was also bare; there were no doors in or out.

I stood up and walked over to the wall between the window and the fireplace. I thought I remembered something being there. I tapped on it with my knuckles to see if anything would happen. Nothing did.

I made my way to the window and swung a leg over the ledge. A whole town sprawled out below me. A few people strolled around, all dressed in brown. They were just barely bigger than ants from where I was sitting. I pulled my other leg over and started to make my way down the side of the tower. As I climbed down, I thought I heard something in the room, but I was already heading in the opposite direction. Once both of my feet were planted on the ground, the piano began to play, filling the streets with an eerie, melancholic music.

I found a bicycle leaning against the wall in front of me. It was covered in dust and moss. I wiped it away with my hand to reveal shimmering, light blue paint and white seat. It was beautiful. I climbed onto the seat, wrapped my hands around the handlebars, and tentatively pushed off.

The people I passed stepped aside to let me through but otherwise ignored me. I saw the tunnels I had gone through earlier but decided to ride parallel to them instead. This led me down a few twists and turns, up one hill and down another, winding my way around the town as the sun set, until I came to a stop in front of a street fair.

The whole strip had been roped off with string lights. Men on unicycles rode past me as I walked the bike down the street. Sparklers were lit everywhere, and children carried small paper lanterns. The piano music still played over it all. The booths in the middle of the street varied. Some were your typical fair booths, sporting popcorn and funnel cakes. Some purported to be fortune tellers and psychics, with gauzy fabric gathered around them and glittery images of stars and cats printed on the walls. One featured a large, bear-like creature standing with chains wrapped around its neck. It was either fake or stuffed and did not move, but it had its arms lifted menacingly over its head. The lightbulbs that surrounded it were all red.

One booth had a firebreather up on a stage. I stopped for a moment to watch her contort and play with the flames. She let it glide over her lean, tanned body, then lifted it to her mouth. She grinned at me and opened her lips slightly, blowing a kiss towards the flame. It erupted into a fireball, shooting up into the air. She twirled the torch in her hands and shot me another look. This time my heart skipped a beat. Her eyes were black with swirls of red.

I stumbled backwards and got back onto the bike. As I pushed off, I looked around. Nobody else had the panic eyes, at least not yet. I passed more booths with performers and goods. Only one, a jeweler, stopped me. His booth was filled with sparkling gems and dark, shiny metals. I didn't have any money, but the old man held up a finger. One. I could take one item. I let my fingers dance across jade cats, tourmaline stars, and citrine hands, but none really spoke to me. He reached below his table and pulled out a black box lined with dark blue velvet. Inside was an amethyst moon. Small hematite beads lined up the sides of it, with a black cord eventually emerging into a sliding knot. I reached out and gently touched the moon pendant.

Immediately, the world swirled around me, diving in on itself and trembling. I screamed and fell backwards, landing on my butt. When I opened my eyes, I was on a dirt road. The moon above me was full, unlike the crescent that hung on my neck. I stood up and brushed my dress off. It was long and extravagant, not like the shorter dress I had been wearing. Along either side of the road were woods. Brambling blackberry bushes burst through patches between trees and wild roses entangled themselves everywhere else. Fireflies flitted around the road and in the woods, casting little green glows wherever they went. This area felt familiar to me, but I couldn't put a finger on why. I decided to continue down the path, heading away from the moon, to see what was there. As I started to walk, I heard footsteps. When I stopped, they did, too.

I shrugged it off as my own paranoia. I was in a new place that felt eerily familiar, at night, in clothes I did not recognize. Everything was strange.

After a few minutes of walking, I heard the footsteps again. This time, they were accompanied by the crunching of leaves. I turned my head slightly to my left and peeked into the woods. At first I didn't see anything, just trees and other vegetation. Then, between the fireflies and the moon, I saw it- a large, lumbering human-like creature. I took two steps and stopped. It took two steps and stopped. I took one, it took one. I gathered up my dress and started to run. It started to run, as well. I ran faster, though, and eventually lost it. I was tired and there was a bend up in the road. I stopped dead in my tracks. I had an awful feeling about what would happen if I were to turn that corner. Again, the familiarity of the situation washed over me. I also knew I couldn't just stay still, or the thing chasing me would get me.

I twisted the necklace around in my fingers, trying to figure out what to do. As I heard the footsteps approaching, I twisted around, closed my eyes, and took off running in the opposite direction. I felt fingertips brush against my arm as I did so, and I cried out in fear. I ran as hard as I could, but this time, the footsteps were keeping up.

I came to a clearing where the woods ended and found myself standing in front of a cemetery and church to my left, and a field of corn to my right. The wind blew and rustled the corn. The footsteps were catching up. I looked over at the cemetery and quickly decided that I was not about to play hide and seek with this person or thing in a cemetery. That sounded like something straight out of a horror movie. Instead, I decided that hiding in the church would be the best option.

I flung the doors open and ran inside, making a beeline for the altar. I knelt and muttered out the lord's prayer as best as I could remember it. I heard the creature come in and start walking over to me. I said the prayer louder and imagined a large globe of golden light coming out of and surrounding me. Eventually, the presence faded, and I got up and looked back towards the door. There was nothing there.

I quietly closed the doors and examined my surroundings. The pews were filled with hymnals, scattered around carelessly. I started to put them back into their little cubbies as I walked through the space. As I worked, I hummed a little tune I had learned back when I went to church. I hadn't been in a long time. Sometime between realizing I also liked girls and that other people should be treated with love and kindness, I determined that it really wasn't my thing. It didn't stop my more spiritual beliefs from manifesting, but the structural ones that had been drilled into me just couldn't stick.

After the worship area had been tidied, I noticed a door to the left. I opened it and found myself in a Sunday school room. Colorful pictures of bible figures hung on the walls- Noah and his animals, David and Goliath, Daniel and the lions, Joseph and the coat of many colors. They all looked a little sinister in the moonlight, though. There was a table with many small chairs circled around it. Crayons littered the surface. I carefully placed them all back into the bucket that sat in the middle of the table. I saw a large shelf on the wall where a bunch of supplies were kept. I took the bucket to it and placed it next to a stack of felt animals.

Just beyond the shelves, to my right was a stairwell leading down into a basement. It was dark, but I followed the steps down. As I did, that same sinking feeling hit me. There was something really bad down there. I first thought to push past it and see what was there, but the next step felt like a punch in the gut. I started muttering the lord's prayer again and imagining that ball of golden light. Before I could hit the last step, I heard a screech come from the dark room, and I turned and scrambled up the steps. I ran through the Sunday school room, where some small children looked at me with confusion, the sunlight dancing across their faces. I tore through the worship room. The preacher in the pulpit was warning everyone about demons in hell and how everyone worldly was going to go there. I ran past the judging eyes and out the door. As I did, I found myself flung in front of the jewelers booth.

I turned, expecting to see the church behind me, but it was all the same street I was on before. I looked at the jeweler, who kept his same calm demeanor. I touched the amulet around my neck, and he nodded sagely. As his head came up, his eyes flashed black with swirls of red.

I got back onto my bicycle and rode away from the fair, noticing panic eyes in everyone I passed. As I rode, the street grew narrow, the buildings ebbed, and eventually I was on a dirt path like I had been before. This time, I could hear the footsteps and pedaled faster. It didn't make a difference, as the thing kept up with me. I could see the shadow shifting in between the trees. Was this the overwhelming feeling that came with the panic eyes? Was this the creature?

I bicycled as fast as I could, but eventually ended up at that same bend in the road. Again, I felt that something very awful would happen if I kept going, but I also knew that creature was about to catch up to me. I stepped off the bike, tossing it to the side, and turned to face it.

Sure enough, I saw the red and black eyes coming towards me. I dug my feet into the dirt, clenched my fists, and began to focus. I closed my eyes.

"Wake up."

Nothing.

"Wake up."

Leaves crunching nearby

"Wake up!"

Footsteps on the road.

"Wake! Up!"

I opened my eyes.

I was now back in the top of the tower, sitting at the piano once more.

I shot a glance over to the window, where a face with a mess of curls peered in at me.

"I was never here," Ariana said.

"Thank you," I replied.

"Wake up," she responded matter-of-factly.

I watched as she tossed her legs over the side and started to climb down.

I looked back to the piano and picked out a tune.

I felt like I had questions, but I couldn't remember what. I know I wanted to know about the mouse and the panic eyes, but there had been something else, too.

Shrugging it off, I took a deep breath and closed my eyes.

"Wake up."

Eyes opened. Nothing.

"Wake up."

Eyes opened again. Still nothing.

"Wake up!"

I opened my eyes for the third time and found the gaunt young man standing in front of me. He set his hand on my head.

"Wake up," he whispered and let his fingers drip down my face.

I struggled for a moment, but once I felt that cool calm take over me, I relaxed.

"Wake up," he whispered again, running his fingers down my face.

"Wake up."

Chapter Twelve

Wake up, Sam, time to go."

Samantha groaned and looked at her phone. 8 am.

"No," she cried, rolling up into the blankets. "One more hour."

"Come on," Rob cajoled, tugging on her arm. "We need to grab breakfast before we head to the convention."

"Sleep is better than food," she mumbled.

"Well, that's a first," Rob said in mock astonishment.

She pulled her arm back and peered at him over the blankets.

"How are you awake?" she asked. "When did you wake up?"

"About an hour ago," he replied. "I thought I'd let you sleep in a bit. You were having more nightmares last night. I woke you up a few times. Do you remember?"

Samantha shook her head. Truth be told, she didn't remember much of the nightmares she had been having either.

Rob nodded solemnly. "It seemed really rough. We need to make sure you're getting enough food and rest."

"Exactly," Samantha agreed. "Rest."

She buried her head under the covers.

"Nope, food first," Rob reiterated and pulled the covers off of her.

Samantha groaned again but sat up. She and Rob stared at each other a moment, contemplating.

Samantha broke the silence.

"Well, where are we going?"

Rob grinned. "There's my girl. I figured we would try that cafe the driver recommended yesterday."

Samantha nodded and stretched. She stood up and sorted through her clothes. She regretted not buying sweat pants while they were there before. She did find a pair of yoga pants that she could pair with one of tshirts they had bought for Rob the day before. Pleased with this combination, she hopped in the shower and prayed for wakefulness.

"Don't forget, we do have to leave a little early today," Rob called out some time later.

"Why's that?" Samantha asked.

"The after party," Rob replied.

Samantha's blood ran cold. She had forgotten about the after party.

"Don't worry," Rob said, peeking into the shower. "We'll leave extra early so you have time to prepare."

Samantha smiled. "Thank you."

Rob kissed her. "Anything for you."

Samantha turned the water off and stepped out into a towel Rob was offering.

She gave him a pout. "Are you sure we can't stay in bed?"

Rob grabbed another towel and began to twist it. "Don't make me!" he cried out.

Samantha laughed and dodged a pop from the towel.

"Get dressed," Rob said, laughing and chasing her while snapping the towel in his hands.

After more laughter and some clothes and make up later, they were on their way to the cafe.

Samantha was delighted to see how small and carefully decorated it was. Ivy ran over everything, large beanbags sat on the floor where one might expect booths, and the bar stools had thin, windy legs on them. They were seated at two of the beanbags facing a low table. They ordered a variety of pastries and some coffee.

The food was not a disappointment at all. Each pastry was baked to perfection. Jams and creams were liberally used as was chocolate ganache. Samantha was glad she had ordered a black coffee, because anything else may have been too much.

This was the best breakfast Samantha had attended in a long time, not just because of the food, but because of the time with Rob.

He was excitedly telling her about the game he was going to stream for the guys he had met the night before, what panels he was looking forward to, how his stream was going to be updated when they got home. He was like a small child with a puppy.

Samantha smiled and sipped her coffee. It was good to see him this happy. There had been other times where stress had clearly worn him ragged, but this was like a whole new Rob compared to those. He couldn't stop talking or smiling. His hands waved and danced while he spoke, weaving their own story.

"What about you?" he asked. "What are you planning to do with your stream?"

"Oh, I don't know," she replied. "Maybe some art stuff."

Rob nodded. "It would be nice to see you get back into art," he said. "You've always had a knack for it."

Samantha blushed. "Thank you."

"If you need some layouts done, I know a few artists who could help out," he continued. "I know one who did Cassie and Bella's layouts in just 2 or 3 days."

Samantha blushed again, but not with pleasure. "I'll think about it," she said tersely before taking a sip of her coffee. Bella was another rising star in their scene who was getting far too close with Rob. She ended up blocking her on social media just to avoid watching the two swap pictures all day long.

"You should," Rob said, seemingly oblivious to Samantha's train of thought. "She's a woman herself and very big into the whole women in men's spaces scene."

"That's cool," Samantha remarked flatly.

"Cassie and Bella? Maybe he's preparing you for tonight," a voice chimed in.

"No, no, no, Bella's in Greece for the weekend. Remember the bikini picture she posted?" another corrected.

Samantha waved her hand as if shooing a fly. Rob raised an eyebrow. She caught his eye.

"Woo, this coffee is warming me up," she said, fanning her face. "This was really good food."

Rob's eyes narrowed.

"Don't tell me you still have a thing about Cassie? Is that what happened yesterday? Why you disappeared?" he asked.

Samantha's eyebrows shot up. "What? No! I saw an interesting booth, and when I turned around you were gone."

Rob sat back. "Uh huh, okay."

"Why would I be worried about Cassie? What she does is her own business," Samantha continued.

"And what is that exactly?" Rob asked.

"You know," Samantha said, "bounce up and down for views, show off her body for likes, play dumb, at least I hope it's an act, play dumb for donations."

Rob set his cup down. "There it is."

"What?" Samantha demanded.

"She's doing a job," Rob said. "That's all. It's a job."

"And I think that's fine," Samantha retorted. "You know I believe sex work is valid."

Rob scoffed, "Sex work?"

"She uses her body to make money off of lonely men," Samantha insisted. "Sex. Work."

Rob shook his head. "I don't know why you have this obsession with her."

"I don't," she declared.

He pointed his finger at her. "You do. You let it dictate your emotions, your actions, everything. You're not in competition with her. Nobody is in competition with anybody. She is just a woman doing a job that she enjoys. She's got her own life and her own problems. She doesn't need some jealous girl being rude to her for no reason."

"I am not jealous," Samantha gasped, "And I have never been rude to her."

"What about yesterday?" Rob asked.

"What about it? She said hi, I didn't recognize her at first, I went to go look at art rather than be in an awkward conversation with someone I barely know."

"That's not how she put it," Rob replied, picking his drink back up.

"Oh, and when did you hear her side of it?" Samantha asked, hostility lacing each word.

"Yesterday, while you were napping," he answered. "She texted me to see if you were feeling okay because you seemed tired when you two talked."

He leaned forward towards Samantha.

"And I know what she meant by 'tired', Sam," he remarked.

Samantha chose not to answer, sipping on her drink instead.

"It's just that it insults me when you do this. Like I don't love you enough? I'm such a shit fiance that I'm going to up and leave you for a girl on the internet? Do you really think that little of me?" he asked.

Samantha shook her head no.

"Then don't act like it," Rob said. "I love you, and I'm not going anywhere. You're beautiful and smart and funny. You're not beneath anyone, but don't use that knowledge to stomp on others. Just live and let live."

Samantha nodded and finished her drink.

"Ready when you are," she said.

Rob rolled his eyes. "Did anything just get through to you?"

"Yes," Samantha insisted. "Thank you for reaffirming everything. It helped a lot."

"Liar," a thin voice hissed.

Rob smiled. "Good. Now let's have a great day, okay?"

He finished his drink and gave Samantha a peck on the cheek.

They paid for their food and made their way to the convention center. They agreed to meet at the big entrance map at three, then parted ways.

As Rob walked off to find the game developers he had met earlier, Samantha decided to do another walk around the floor. Her next panel didn't start for another hour. It was much busier that day than the day before. Cosplayers roamed in packs, booths had employees standing to the side, handing off free items, and a few more vendors had joined the hall.

She passed by at least six different dice makers before spotting a jewelry booth. It had the usual inventory- dice earrings, perler bead pendants, hearts and potion bottles. Something had caught her eye, though. It was a rack of black corded necklaces. Some had silver wolves, others held jade cats, one had an emerald eye wrapped in wire. What Samantha saw and was now holding in her hand, was an amethyst moon with hematite beads. She couldn't explain the draw, just that it seemed familiar.

"She called to ya," the man behind the booth said.

Samantha looked at him and nodded. "I guess so," she said.

"Tell ya what," he said, tugging at his jeans. "That one's traveled with me to three different shows. I can't seem to shake it. It's just gone on clearance."

He took the necklace and marked it down ten dollars. Samantha's eyes widened.

"Wow, thank you!" she said, reaching for her wallet.

"No worries, like I said, she called to ya," he commented.

Samantha paid for the necklace and immediately put it on. It fit perfectly.

She took the jeweler's card and moved on to the next section.

She perused the miniatures for a bit, combed through a booth with vintage video games, and checked out a few board games. At one point Jason and Todd walked by. They said hi and asked if Samantha was going to be at the dinner. She told them she would be, and the party too, and they seemed happy to hear it. She asked if they were going to any of the panels; they shook their heads. They weren't really interested in anything being offered, they explained, and they had a lot of networking to do.

As they wandered off, Samantha checked the time and was shocked to see that the panel she wanted to see had started five minutes ago. She rushed through the crowd of people, up the escalator, and to the hall where all the panels were being held.

She quietly snuck in and stood awkwardly in the back of the room. It sounded like they were just starting to discuss the topic. For the next hour, she listened to the panelists discuss studies being conducted into how video games were being used to treat depression, anxiety, and ptsd. They wove in stories from their own lives about how video games had helped them through difficult times and encouraged the audience to engage with them outside of the panel. One was a representative from the group who had created the quiet space the elf girl had told Samantha about earlier. She spoke at length about how the gaming community could be used as a force of good to help uplift its members. She had many examples from the group she was with and the responses they had received from their work at conventions and gaming tournaments.

Samantha found the whole event fascinating. She had held a deep love for psychology from an early age. She was often the secret keeper and the pseudo-counselor to her friends and family growing up. While she did not pursue it in college, she still found herself drawn to it. Combining that interest with another, as this panel did, made her heart leap with joy. She had forgotten about the anxiety she had faced earlier. Instead, she took pictures of the end slide, which listed a series of links to studies and games involved in the panel, and planned to get involved as much as possible.

In order to immerse herself further, and to kill time before her next panel, Samantha decided to check out the quiet space. It was just across the hall, and the moment the door opened, she was struck with just how quiet it actually was. People snoozed on beanbags, colored at tables, paced with earbuds in, and sat reading comics and books.

She looked around in awe, then made her way to one of the tables. She slid into a chair and pulled out the notebook she had bought the day before. Fishing a pencil out of a bucket on the table, she settled in and started to draw. As she did, the voices started to swirl in her mind, directing her on what to draw and how to do so. She chose to work on some characters for a comic she had come up with a few months prior.

She was working on the third character when a lady walked over and stooped in front of her. She was older, with a sweater and a beaded chain on her glasses, standing out from the sea of tshirts and hoodies.

"May I see?" she whispered.

Samantha nodded and turned the book around.

The lady flipped through the pages, studying each character carefully before turning the book back.

"You are very talented," she whispered. "Are these from a series?"

Samantha nodded again. "My own," she whispered back.

The woman raised her eyebrows and her eyes sparkled. "That's amazing," she said in a hushed tone. "You're very creative. Keep it up!"

With that, she shuffled off to one of the people with the earbuds, asking to listen to their music. They obliged and had a small dance party. Samantha smiled to herself. That lady was doing a very uplifting thing, and she hoped that she knew how appreciated she was.

Samantha went back to drawing, finishing up five characters in total, before gathering her things and heading to the next panel. This one would be about gender in gaming, and she was looking forward to hearing all of the different perspectives that would come into play. As she entered the room, she looked up at the stage and froze. Cassie was there, giggling and whispering into the ear of the guy next to her. She was wearing a bodycon dress patterned to look like a popular video game creature and tall high heeled boots, not practical for walking around on concrete all day.

Samantha thought about leaving but decided against it. She was empowered now. She would not miss the panel she was interested in just because Cassie was in it. Besides, it may be interesting to see her perspective on the issue. She took a seat toward the middle of the room and waited for the panel to start.

A moment later, a voice called out, "This seat taken?"

She looked up to find Rob grinning at her. She patted the seat next to her.

"Go right ahead. I didn't think you'd be here. Didn't you have some networking to do?"

He sat down and stretched an arm around her. "I did, and it went really well. I promised Cass I would check out one of her panels, and I figured you would be here. It seemed like your kind of topic."

Samantha nodded and turned towards the platform again. Cassie's eyes were scanning the crowd, and they settled on her. She got a big smile on her face and waved.

Before Samantha could react, Rob waved back. Cassie blew him a kiss, then continued to look around the room.

Samantha wriggled down into her seat and wondered if it were too late to go back to the quiet room and show the nice lady her drawings again.

The panel itself did turn out to be very interesting. Rather than sticking with the tried and true "girls versus boys", they also discussed the nonbinary experience, as well as the traditionally feminine girls as compared to more traditional masculine girls. The contrast of their experiences in chat was very pronounced but still carried shared strains of hatred and taunting. The panelists did clarify that there were many servers they played on where this wasn't an issue but were careful not to discount those other experiences. There was also discussion of the standard "boy or girl" option at the beginning of games, games that subverted that trope, and others that ditched the standard altogether.

Everytime Cassie spoke, Samantha's stomach dipped. Knowing that Rob had shown up just for her, it ate at her, and the kiss just set it all off. Part of her wanted to jump up and accuse Cassie of cementing those gender roles and expectations into place, and part of her was horrified at that.

"She's that girl, the one who flirts her way through games," a voice hissed.

"Hey, if it works, it works. Don't hate the player," another chirped.

When the panel ended, Samantha made a beeline for the door. Rob grabbed her arm.

"Wait up, we should talk to Cassie, congratulate her on a good panel."

"Okay, then I'll meet you downstairs," she said, pulling her arm away.

She rushed to the escalator and closed her eyes on the way down. There was no way she could handle that, not in that moment, anyway.

She opened her eyes in time to step off and head towards the large schedule that greeted everyone. She eyed the rest of the day's events, knowing she would miss them but curious as to what they were anyway. Eventually, Rob walked up.

"Ready to go?" he asked.

Samantha nodded, and they left. The car ride to the house was quiet, and Samantha guessed that she had rubbed Rob the wrong way at the panel.

"Oh, well," a relaxed voice piped up, "his loss."

"Just focus on the party," a stern voice iterated. "Delicious dinner, then fun party. You've got this."

Samantha nodded. She did have this.

They went inside, and Samantha took a quick shower. She shuffled into her red dress, bending and squeezing and holding her breath in places until it was on and zipped. It did cling quite a bit, but again, Rob seemed to like it.

She went ahead and put on the nails she had bought and started to do her makeup. She did get a bit of thrill out of the lipstick she had purchased. It was the perfect, velvety shade of crimson and went spectacularly with her dress. Her hair took longer as she toyed with pulling it up, leaving it down, pulling it back on the sides. She ended up curling the front pieces away from her face, and curling the sides towards it.

Finally, she had Rob help her put on the diamond necklace he had gotten her after their engagement. It was the perfect finishing touch. She looked herself over in the mirror and reluctantly gave it approval. She still wasn't happy with her appearance, but this was leaps and bounds over her usual look.

She slipped into some heels, made sure her id was slipped into her phone's pocket, and then they stepped outside to meet their rideshare driver.

Chapter Thirteen

I opened my eyes. I was lying on my back in a large comfortable bed. Silky white swaths of fabric swayed from the tall wooden posts at each corner. The soft sheets and pillowcases were also a pristine white, a similar tint as the linen pants and tank top I wore. One either side of the bed was a nightstand in the same dark wood the bed was made of. I slowly sat up and looked around.

To my left, the blue walls of the room dipped into a smaller, darker enclosure, which housed a rusting spiral staircase. To my right, a door stood ajar, with a filing cabinet peeking out from behind it. Past the door was a hallway; stairs with a dark red runner led down to the floor below. Right in front of me, though, is what caught my breath.

A large window with scrollwork on the sill sat curtainless on the wall before me. I stood up and made my way over to it. Outside, water crashed on a beach full of light sand. Just past the sand, a forest rose up. Clouds gathered overhead, but it was not stormy. No birds flew by, and nobody was on the beach. The scene was still with the exception of the rolling waves giving the water the visage of breath.

I stared out of the window for a long time, letting myself get lost in the view.

Slowly, a noise started to waft up from downstairs, the sound of people speaking in hushed tones. I turned from the window and craned my neck to peer down the stairs, but all I saw was the wall. As I stepped past the door to the filing cabinets, I heard someone call my name.

Chapter Fourteen

S am, wake up, we're here."

Samantha opened her eyes and stretched. The driver caught her glance in the rearview mirror and chuckled.

"You look like you needed that!" he said.

Samantha nodded sleepily. She was always falling asleep, no matter where she was. It could be embarrassing at times, but she figured if she didn't need the sleep, she wouldn't fall asleep.

Rob helped her out of the car.

"You are so beautiful," he said.

Samantha blushed. "Thank you," she replied.

Rob smiled. "Just telling the truth."

He led her to the front door of the restaurant, where the host brought them to their table. A few of their friends were already seated. Now Samantha felt like she belonged. Everyone had on suits and ties or cocktail dresses.

She was seated next to a gentleman she didn't recognize in a dark blue scroll vest. Across from her sat one of Rob's close friends, Derek. She hadn't spoken to him or his wife, Kara, too many times, but he was a familiar face. Jason and Todd sat across from each other at the very end of the table. They leaned forward and waved at her. She smiled and waved back.

The waiter stopped by after Rob was seated and asked for their drink preference. Rob, true to himself, ordered an ale. Samantha, trying to look cultured, browsed the wine list carefully before ordering what she was always going to get: a cabernet sauvignon. The table was fairly quiet, broken into separate hushed conversations at first. Once everyone got their drinks, the mood began to lift, and everyone became roped into one of two conversations. On Jason and Todd's side of the table, there was animated talk about a new game releasing that had a female antagonist that had created buzz around the gaming world. On Rob and Samantha's side, discussion about the military charity that was at the convention arose with one of the dinner guests, a veteran, regaling the others about his time stationed abroad.

When it came time to order food, Samantha actually did meticulously study the menu. She wanted to get something that tasted good but would look chic and small on the plate. She found a chicken dish that sounded promising and ordered that. She carefully listened to the other women order, and they all went for seafood. She cringed a little inside. She couldn't stand fish. She could keep them in tanks, view them at aquariums, even catch them on a line, but eat them? Never.

The waiter brought over another round of drinks and poured Samantha another glass of wine. She sipped it nonchalantly, trying to look like she was effortlessly social. In reality, she could feel her stomach clenching up.

"Your boobs are out," a voice hissed at her. "Put them back. Should have brought a sweater, whore."

"You look great!" another voice cheered. "Not as good as the other women, but great!"

"Yeah," the first voice added, "considering you've got a good fifty pounds on the heaviest one."

"And that afterparty is going to be something else," the chipper voice said.

"Oh, for sure," the hissing voice cackled. "Sloppy drunk and crying in the bathroom, I'm calling it."

"She won't be!" the chipper voice said. "It's going to be awesome! Everyone there will be nice. She'll have a few drinks and chat everyone up."

"Oh, like she's doing now? She's practically molded herself to the chair. You think the waiter is going to keep pouring her wine by the glass or eventually feel bad enough to hand her the bottle?"

"That dress is a bit tight," another voice chimed in. "Hopefully the food doesn't cause your stomach to bloat."

"Even without the bloat," the hissing voice said, "your stomach is still sticking out. You thought the boobs and that lumpy butt of yours was bad? You should see that gut straining against the fabric. Nightmare fuel."

Samantha drained her second glass of wine and tried to become absorbed in the conversation. Her dad was a veteran, so she had a few pieces of input here and there. To her relief, they accepted what she was saying and didn't ignore her or tease her. The conversation flowed easily, and eventually, their food did arrive.

Samantha watched as entire, large fish were sat down on the table with large mixing bowls of salad and bread. Huge slabs of steak made their way over with baked potatoes the size of newborns. She was equal parts excited and scared for her dinner. She wanted to look dainty, but it seemed like this restaurant was not the place for it.

The waiter sat her large bowl of salad down first. Then came the plate of chicken. Samantha stared at it, bewildered. It looked to either be a very small chicken breast or half of one, with a thin ribbon of sauce run over it with three small raviolis on the side.

She looked around as everyone started to pick up their silverware. Her plate was very small in comparison to all the others.

The waiter came back around and poured her another glass of wine. He gave her a knowing look as he did so. This probably wasn't the first time he had seen this play out.

Ignoring the chatter in her head, she sat her napkin in her lap and began to cut the chicken into pieces. She managed to get five small bites separated out on the plate and smeared each of them in as much sauce as possible. At least she had the salad, she figured.

While everyone began to eat, Derek and Kara took advantage of the quiet, stood up, and got everyone's attention.

"Thank you so much for coming," Derek said, "And thank you, Todd and Jason, for putting up your suite for the party after this."

Everyone applauded. Jason blushed, and Todd dipped his head in a little bow.

"We wanted to gather everyone in person," Derek continued, "So that when we're in game, we know each other's faces, which means no more waifus for you, Scott!"

Everyone laughed, and the man in the blue vest grinned and gave a thumbs down.

"You're not my mom, Derek!" he said with a fake pout. Samantha gathered that he was the one who always played as a spunky, lithe anime girl. She ran into him in a zombie game once and was more than a little shocked at the deep baritone that came out of the small, pink haired cherub in front of her. So that was what he looked like, handsome with a dark beard and a head of equally dark curls. She wasn't sure how she would have pictured him but it wouldn't have been that.

"We also wanted to introduce you to another gamer," Kara added. She raised her water glass and placed a hand on her stomach.

Everyone gasped and started to cheer. Congratulations were given around the table, and a toast was raised. Immediately, the conversation turned towards children. Samantha took this opportunity to dive into her salad, carefully chewing each leaf and vegetable. She didn't have children of her own and didn't see that happening for at least a few more years. She sipped her wine and savored the way it buzzed in her head.

At one point, Scott turned towards Samantha and motioned at her with his fork.

"So what about you and Rob?" he asked. "Thinking of kids anytime soon?"

Samantha finished off her wine. "You know, we've talked about it," she said.

His eyebrows raised. "Yeah?"

Samantha nodded. "Maybe sometime next year," she let slip.

His eyes twinkled and he raised his glass. Samantha awkwardly raised a water glass to meet it and took a sip. She wasn't sure why she said that, but it felt right at the time.

Conversation started to die down as people finished their dinner. The waiter asked about dessert, then split the check up for everyone. Some of the wives and girlfriends made plans to go to a bar further into the city. Samantha declined, and everyone laughed.

Rob slung an arm around her. "That's my girl, one of the guys."

They all laughed again, and Samantha smiled at everyone, wondering if the blush across her face was from the attention or the wine.

Once the checks were paid, everyone gathered outside, waiting for cars to take them to their parties. Samantha gave Kara a hug and wished her the best with everything.

"You, too," she replied with a wink. "You know, in a few months."

Samantha blinked. Had she heard the conversation with Scott? Was she referring to something else? She internally shrugged and chalked it up to some forgotten discussion, like many others.

The cars arrived, and Samantha found herself packed in between Rob and Todd while Jason rode shotgun.

"We've got a full bar," Todd explained enthusiastically. "We have a camera set up, ready to stream. We've got a gaming pc up and running as well as some table top stuff. We figured we'll rotate the host every hour or so until the night winds down."

"Can I do the first leg?" Rob asked, getting excited.

"Absolutely!" Todd said, giving him a high five.

They began to talk about a science fiction game they had early access to, and how it would be the perfect game to start the night out. As they dove into lore and space ship details, Samantha found her head growing fuzzy. Her eyes unfocused, and she couldn't feel her lips or fingertips. She stared blankly ahead and let their words swirl around her. These were the same conversations she got looped into at home. This game was a particular favorite of Rob's, and he was always regaling her with some new detail or bit of news. At one point, Jason turned around to join in the conversation. He made eye contact with Samantha and furrowed his brow in concern. She refocused and waved a hand at him. He nodded and moved on.

The car pulled up in front of the hotel. They clambered out and made their way to the elevator. When Todd unlocked the door, Samantha couldn't help but be impressed. The kitchenette did indeed have a full bar's worth of liquor stocked on the counter. They explained that there was some beer in the fridge, but not much. The entire living room section was lit up with LEDs that snaked around the ceiling, and sure enough, there was a pc set up on the desk with multiple cameras around the room. A laptop running a dozen different programs and pulling the camera feeds sat on the table next to the couch. Bowls of chips and popcorn littered the area, placed strategically next to card decks and board games. The bathroom sat between the two bedrooms and had extra toilet paper and towels stacked up in preparation for extra guests. Samantha wasn't sure if the second room housed extra guests, or if Todd and Jason were still laying low.

Immediately, Jason began to pour drinks, and the second and third groups from dinner piled in. Samantha found herself with a large solo cup full of tequila and orange juice in the living room helping Rob and Todd set up the stream. Social media announcements were made, and soon after, chat was rolling on the side of the laptop. Some mentioned they were on their way over, some asked for an invite, and others were happy just to join the party remotely.

Rob fired up the science fiction game and started piloting a large ship, while one of the cameras focused on a card game getting started by four other guys. Samantha sat awkwardly on the couch and watched what chat was saying. Todd shifted the cameras around so it was on them. He told Samantha to wave and introduced her to the people online. She smiled, and comments started to pour in.

"Are you Robket's girlfriend?"

"I saw you at the convention earlier! How are those ears holding up?"
"Who is this?"

"I thought Todd was gay?"

"Is that your sister?"

"What's your channel, sweetheart?"

"Get back to the cards, Todd."

"Who cut your hair and why was it with a chainsaw?"

"Bewbs. Lol."

"Seriously, is this Robket's girlfriend?"

"I thought they broke up."

"Who's the girl?"

"How's the card game coming along? Who's winning?"

Todd switched the camera over to the kitchen where Jason toasted the online viewers. More people arrived, and Samantha got up to get a refill. Jason seemed to read her pinched expression quite clearly and made this drink more tequila than orange juice. She sipped on the drink and talked to him for a bit. As it turned out, there were a few guys who were crashing in the suite with them. They had saved up or raised enough money to get tickets to the convention but not enough to cover a room on their own.
"That sounds about right, you big softie," Samantha teased Jason, feeling a bit emboldened by the alcohol.

Jason blushed. "You have to do what's right, you know? People are people, and you have to help one another."

Samantha nodded sagely and had him top off her drink.

She wandered back into the living room, where Rob waved her down. She stooped near his chair, and he gave her a quick kiss on the cheek. "EW!" rang out around the crowd followed by laughter.

Todd pointed a finger at the camera on the table. "See!" he shouted, "I told you!"

Samantha made her way to the couch. The conversation had devolved into whether Rob was single or not. She was surprised; she didn't think that Rob kept their relationship a secret. Everyone at the convention knew about her. Why was this particular chat confused? It settled uneasily into her stomach.

She quickly turned away and began talking with a couple of journalists. They had been covering a horror survival game she had been interested in, and they had all the juicy details. At one point, someone grabbed her cup and brought it back full of tequila and orange juice. The voices swirled, reminding Samantha of basic party rules, never drinking from an unobserved cup, but she shrugged them off. This was a safe place, and Jason was the one making drinks. She continued her conversation and sipped on her drink. Her stomach started to rumble, but she ignored it. She wasn't about to eat out of bowls that everyone's grubby hands had been in.

Suddenly, the crowd started cheering, and the men she was talking to raised their cups and whooped excitedly. Feeling comfortably buzzed, she did the same and turned around. Her stomach dropped, and she nearly dropped her cup.

Cassie had entered.

She was wearing a tiny black pleated skirt with an even smaller black crop top. She bounced in on stilettos taller than any heel Samantha owned. She ran up to Jason, gave him a big hug and a kiss on the cheek and had him pour her a vodka tonic. She made her way around the crowd like that, giving everyone a hug and a quick kiss. Instinctively, Samantha took a few steps back toward the bathroom. She wasn't sure if Cassie saw her, but she passed by her regardless. Samantha watched as she turned, put her hands in the air, and screamed, "ROBKET!".

Rob turned from his game and opened his arms. She trotted over to him, wrapped him in a big hug, and gave him a big kiss on the top of the head. Rob said something into the mic and gestured towards Cassie, who shifted her weight to the side and gave a peace sign. Samantha couldn't read the chat from where she was, but she could see it scrolling at lightspeed. She downed her cup and went to get another.

Jason gave her a weird look but poured it for her.

"Are you okay, Sam," he asked with concern.

"Hmm? Oh, yeah, I'm fine. Just tired," she said out of habit.

"Do you want something to eat? It didn't look like you got much at dinner."

She caught sight of Cassie dancing out of the corner of her eye. Her stomach was flat, and her hips were undulating two inches from Rob's face. He had moved from the gaming seat to the couch.

"Nah," she replied. "It was actually really filling. They stuffed those ravioli's with lots of fiber or something."

Jason nodded slowly. "Okay, just let me know if you change your mind," he said.

Samantha returned the nod and sauntered back into the living room. Cassie stopped dancing and sat down on the couch, too, leaning against Rob with her legs across Todd's lap. The camera was on her, and she was talking back and forth with the chat. Samantha swallowed the lump in her throat and walked over, planning on tapping Rob on the shoulder and signaling them to go.

"It's a huge party!" Cassie said into the mic. "Wish you were here, Carlos!"

She blew a kiss at the camera, then read some more messages.

"Have I enjoyed the con? Yes! Everyone has been so nice to me! And I've been able to meet so many of you in real life! It's a dream come true!" she cooed.

Samantha gagged a little and took another sip of her drink. Before she could lean over, Cassie laughed.

"It is a sausage party, Carmen. I'm, like, the only girl here!"

Samantha's blood ran cold. Her face flushed, and the hand around her drink trembled. She looked up at the laptop and saw the scene reflected in the screen: Rob and Todd looking relaxed, Cassie with her skirt bunched up to her hip, leaning forward towards the camera, and Samantha, standing with a horrified expression behind the couch. Without a word, she spun on her heel and went back into the kitchen.

She finished her drink, and, after nobody came to find her, decided she would get another. At this point, Jason had taken a break from serving and was in the living room next to the card game. Samantha grabbed the tequila bottle and poured a straight drink into the solo cup, nearly to the top.

The night began to blur and whenever Cassie entered her periphery, Samantha would scurry off somewhere else. She continued to top her cup off with tequila whenever she could sneak it. Finally, she was caught by Jason, pouring the last few drops into her cup.

"What are you doing, Sam? You have had enough!"

Samantha felt tears begin to rush down her face.

"It's not enough, Jason," she slurred. "It's never enough."

"What's not? What has gotten into you?"

"She's not the only girl at the party, you know!"

Jason looked confused.

"You think everything's good, because you have Todd. You don't care about the cam girls, but I do! Because Rob does. He cares a lot."

She started sobbing. Jason took the cup out of her hand and herded her to the bathroom. Once they got there, he closed the door and put his hands on her shoulders.

"Sam, what is going on?"

"Rob is in love with Cassie!"

Jason rolled his eyes. "I hardly think that is the case."

"It's true! He wants her bad. He thinks she's hot and sexy, and he doesn't want me anymore," Samantha cried.

Jason wiped the tears away from her eyes. "That's not true, dear."

"You saw them! You know!"

He swallowed. "Well, you know, that's just a thing. Think of it this way- he doesn't take her home. He takes you home!"

He smiled, thinking he had made a great point. Samantha started to cry harder.

"Only because I'm there," she said. "If I weren't there he'd take her home. I ruin everything!"

"You're stupid," a voice hissed.

"I'm so stupid," she lamented.

"And fat and ugly," it continued.

"And fat and ugly," she sobbed.

"Everyone loves Cassie and hates you. You should just die," it whispered.

"Everyone loves her, and they hate me, and I should just, should just, should just," she wailed.

Todd poked his head in.

"Everything okay?"

Jason shook his head and pointed at Samantha, who was sitting on the bathroom floor, her cup spilled and forgotten beside her. With each sob, her breasts threatened to flee her dress, she had somehow stained the hem, and her hair was frizzed up in every direction around her face.

Todd nodded and stepped out.

Jason smoothed her hair and cooed at her. "You know none of that is true."

She screamed and began to sob again.

"I just hate her so much," she admitted, feeling the energy leave her body as she said it.

"Don't say that," Jason chided.

"I do. I hate her looks, I hate the way she acts, I hate all the people slobbering all over her, I hate the attention, I hate her!"

The bathroom door swung open, and a livid Rob stood in the center of the doorway.

"We're going home, Sam," he said sternly.

Samantha shook her head. "No."

Rob grabbed her arm and yanked her up off the floor. "We're going. Now."

Samantha saw a flurry of faces and immediately bucked up. She wiped her tears off her face, smoothed her hair, and straightened her dress.

People went up to Rob and asked if he was leaving early. Rob chuckled and shyly said he was. Samantha tried to turn back to the bathroom, but Rob's grip on her arm tightened.

"I'm sorry guys," he said to the murmuring crowd, "I'll be back first thing in the morning for donuts and discussion, I promise!"

"As long as you bring the booze," Todd called out.

Rob grinned and nodded. The crowd cheered.

He turned and dragged Samantha out of the suite. She searched the faces frantically but didn't see Cassie.

They got to the elevator, and he calmly hit the button.

"Where's she?" Samantha slurred quietly.

"She left," Rob replied coldly.

"Good," Samantha said.

Rob bit his lip and tapped his foot. The elevator opened, and he gave her a push towards it.

"In!" he ordered.

Samantha raised her hands up and stumbled in. The ride down was quiet, as was waiting on the car.

When it arrived, Rob helped pour her into the backseat and took the front passenger side. Samantha's thoughts ran wild as they rode. What had she done wrong? Why was Rob upset?

The driver asked if they were there for the convention, and Rob explained they were and began to talk about his channel. Samantha looked out the window while he went on about gaming and streaming. Even now, he was all business.

She looked down at her arm expecting to see marks but found nothing. She was surprised. She had a boyfriend once who left marks on her all the time. Rob was clearly mad at her. Why didn't she have any marks? He had held onto her arm so tightly. She felt a sob welling up but held it in. She was in so much trouble.

They made it to the house, and Rob helped her out of the car. The driver wished them the best and asked for Rob's business card. He gave him one and explained that Samantha would have one soon, once she started her channel. They waved goodnight, and the car drove off. Rob put a hand on her back and guided her into the house.

He opened the door and helped her inside. As soon as her shoes came off, she felt it. A watering in her mouth, a clenching in her throat, and a gushing in her stomach.

She made it as far as the kitchen trash can.

Chapter Fifteen

Is she okay?" Eric asked.

"What the fuck do you think?" Ariana replied. "You saw how much she drank!"

"Just asking! Because I care!" he said defensively.

"Oh, and I don't?" Ariana yelled.

"I didn't see you stopping her!"

"Neither did you!"

"Stop it, both of you," Thomas chided.

"She did it herself. She realized what a stupid ugly useless piece of trash she was, and it was just too much," Charity butted in.

"You take that back," Ariana said. "Take it back now!"

"No! It's true!" Charity cried out.

A wailing sound began to rise.

"Oh, great, you woke her up," Eric said.

"She was going to wake up anyways," Charity huffed.

The wailing grew louder, and they all winced.

"This was a failure on all parts," Thomas said. "What we have to do now is protect her from Rob."

"You don't think he'll do anything?" Eric asked in hushed tones.

"I don't know," Thomas replied. "He was pretty mad, anything is possible."

"I'll take care of it," Ariana stated firmly.

"I think that's probably for the best," Thomas agreed. "I will keep an eye on everything, just in case."

The wailing hit a crescendo and broke out into sobs.

"Ugh, I hate her," Charity groaned.

"We know," Eric retorted, "But it's not going to stop anytime soon."

"Let's find her and make it stop!" Charity argued.

"No," Thomas said. "That's not how this works."

The sobbing continued as Charity and Thomas began to bicker.

"Shut up!" Samantha yelled, right before she puked again.

Rob came back downstairs with a scrunchie and pulled her hair back. Before she could thank him, her head was back in the trash can, and she was heaving even harder than before. Once she stopped, she turned around. Rob was sitting in the living room, staring at her coldly. He waved to a chair sitting next to a table upon which sat a glass of water and a couple tabs of ibuprofen.

Samantha started towards it, and he stopped her.

"Take the can with you," he said.

She nodded and dragged it behind her. She awkwardly took the pills and gulped down half the water. She leaned back in the chair and looked at Rob.

"Well, are you going to say something?" she asked.

"What's there to say?" he replied. "You embarrassed me in front of everyone, friends, colleagues, important people, everyone. You could have ruined my career, permanently, and you made Cassie run off in tears!"

Samantha laughed. "Good, fuck her."

Rob stood up and threw a pillow against the couch.

"No, Sam, fuck you!"

Samantha blinked and looked at him.

"You had a problem this whole time, and you didn't say a word. You could have told me you weren't okay to come, and we would have been fine. Why did you come here? You knew how this would play out, but you insisted."

Samantha shook her head, but Rob continued.

"What, you didn't trust me? You thought there was something going on? Then say it to my face!"

"It's not about you," she whispered.

"Well, it must be, since you said as much at the party!" he yelled. "Todd told me everything, not that I couldn't hear it from where I was sitting."

A cold chill ran through Samantha.

"So, she-"

"Heard everything? Yeah. She went to check on you after realizing you were at the party and heard you say all that nasty shit. I am so embarrassed, Sam, I can't even express to you how ashamed I am."

Samantha began to cry.

"Oh no," Rob said, "It's too late for that. I would say an entire bottle of tequila too late."

"I'm sorry," she wailed.

"Sorry? You're sorry? Now you're sorry? Too. Late."

She sobbed and tried to get up from the chair. Rob gently pushed her back down into it.

"You don't get to be sorry, not after that. What am I supposed to tell people in the morning? How am I supposed to clear things up with everyone? The amount of damage control I have to do is extraordinary, not to mention how I'm supposed to approach Cassie."

He swore under his breath and pulled his phone out of his pocket.

Samantha cried and hiccuped. "Are you texting her?"

Rob glared at her, and she started to sob again. He began to tap away at his phone, then put it away again. He stomped upstairs, and Samantha turned to throw up again.

He came back down with a blanket and a pillow and threw them on the couch.

Samantha shook her head. "No, Rob, please."

He shook his finger at her. "You did this."

"I didn't mean it," she cried.

"In vino veritas," he replied. "There is truth in wine. You meant every word of it."

Samantha started crying again.

"Are you done puking?" he asked.

She nodded, and he picked up the garbage can.

"Upstairs," he ordered.

Samantha shook her head. "No, please."

"Upstairs," he said again.

She cried harder and began to stumble up the stairs. Laying on the bed was a baggy shirt and a pair of shorts. He set the can next to the bed and helped her with the zipper on the back of her dress. She sobbed the entire time.

Once she was dressed for bed, he helped her wipe the makeup off her face and brush her teeth. Not a single word was spoken. He took her from the bathroom, got her to lay down on her side, and tucked her into bed. His phone buzzed, and he pulled it out to look at it.

"Is it her?" she hiccupped.

He paused and looked at her. He searched for the right words, appalled. He waved the phone in her direction.

"You need to see a fucking therapist."

With that, he turned the lights out and went downstairs.

Samantha pulled her knees up to her chest and cried.

"Are you okay, little one?" a kind voice asked.

"Shut up," she wept.

CHAPTER SIXTEEN

Samantha tossed and turned, in and out of sleep. Every few minutes, she leaned over the edge of the bed to heave into the garbage can. The room swirled around her menacingly, leering over her retching body. She couldn't feel her hands or her face and wondered aloud if she may have alcohol poisoning.

Rob came upstairs only once, with a glass of water, to ask if she needed to go to the hospital. She shook her head no and begged him to talk to her. He set the glass down and went back downstairs. She stumbled out of bed to go after him, but the stairs writhed beneath her, and she was afraid of falling. She collapsed back into the blankets and shuddered, chills taking over her body.

They had never fought like this. They had their fair share of arguments, but never had Rob slept in a separate room. She had been very drunk before, but he was always right next to her, making sure she was okay. She tried piecing together the night's events but found that chunks of it were missing. This could have been due to the alcohol, or those memories could have been lost to the swirl of voices haranguing her.

"You did it this time!"

"Stupid, fat, ugly girl!"

"You need help."

She put her hands over her ears and screamed in frustration. This was cut off by another strong heave from the bottom of her stomach. At this point, there was nothing left inside, but her body demanded it be rid of any trace of alcohol.

She sank back down onto the pillow and let her eyes close momentarily. The bed rocked side to side, but when she paced her breathing with it, it didn't make her feel as nauseous. She started to drift off to sleep when a loud thump caused her eyes to snap back open.

She was on her side, facing the stairs. A bit of light from the tv crept up and cast a small glow into the room. She tried to lift herself up on one arm.

She was paralyzed.

Samantha panicked, trying to scream, to alert Rob to what was going on. Nothing came out. Her eyes darted frantically around the room, looking for anything that could help or comfort her. That's when she saw it.

Slowly, over the edge of the bed, the tips of jet black fingers crept. They tapped the top of the mattress slowly, stopping to caress the sheets. Eventually, the whole hand, entirely raven in color, emerged and gestured towards her. Samantha tried to shake her head and scream again, but she found herself frozen still.

The hand splayed itself on the bed, then another rose to join it. The fingers massaged the area, like they were looking for something. Samantha knew she needed to get out. She focused on wiggling her index finger, trying to tap back at the sable hands. It started to twitch just a little, and she heard a squeaking noise. The palms of the hands lifted up, leaving only the fingertips on the bed, poised as if in wait.

A small white mouse emerged from the corner of the bed, scurrying across towards the hands. Its whiskers trembled as it sniffed each finger. The hands scooped the mouse up, running their fingertips over its fur lovingly. They began to move across the bed, towards Samantha's head. The mouse scooted to the edge of the fingers, eagerly squeaking at her. It began to clean its whiskers and rub its own hands together. Memories flooded her of the mouse burrowing into her head, and she began to panic.

As the hands brought it closer, she focused more and more on moving her finger. It wouldn't budge. Gently, the mouse was placed in front of her eyes. It stared at her unnervingly for an eternity, then clambered up her face to her ear. As it began to dig, the hands wriggled their fingers in front of her face, taunting her.

With one great burst of energy, Samantha's body reared up. Her arm swung over her like a hammer, her fist aimed at the hands.

Then, all of a sudden, they were gone. The momentum caused her to tumble over, crashing into the garbage can. She gasped and grappled with it, managing to keep it upright. She looked over at the stairs, waiting for Rob to come up or say something. Not a single sign of life emerged.

She brought her hand up to her ear and found nothing. Again, it was as if nothing had been there at all.

"The mouse?" she asked herself, questioning not only its existence, but its purpose.

"It's always there at the worst possible time," a laid back voice said.

"But why does it burrow? What is it looking for?" she pondered.

"Hard to say, but it really seems to like you," it replied.

Another wave of nausea hit, and she scrambled to place her head over the edge of the can. Again, nothing came of it, but it was better to be safe than sorry.

She shuffled over to the bathroom and turned the shower on. She tried to slip her clothes off, but she still couldn't feel her hands. It took her a long stretch of time, awkwardly tugging and twisting. She then crawled into the shower and laid on the cold tile, letting it cool her body and her head. The water beat down on her and for a moment, she couldn't tell what was shower water and what were tears.

She sobbed, partially for Rob, partially for herself. She had grappled with her mental health all her life, but for someone she loved, someone she was so close to, to tell her she needed therapy, it killed her inside. It felt like a betrayal of trust. She wasn't well, one look would tell anyone that, but it wasn't that bad. She could do better. She could be better.

She began to hiccup and sniffled. That was it. She couldn't open up to Rob any more. She had to take on everything herself quietly, stoically. The only way she could keep him close would be to hold him at arm's length. She also wouldn't be able to be close with anyone else. Everyone was a threat. She couldn't trust anyone, and they certainly would be judging her after everything that had happened. She hiccuped again as she cried. She made her resolution. She was going to be a fortress. Nobody allowed in. She wouldn't be able to let others know how she felt. Rob would only know her as happy, the way he liked it. Clearly the problem was with her and how she perceived things, so she would have to nip it in the bud.

She cried harder as she made these decisions. Voices began to pelt her with questions and accusations, and she batted them all away. This was not the time for input. This was her problem to solve.

She continued to lay in the shower until the water turned cold. She reluctantly pulled herself to her feet and turned it off. The room was spinning less, and she was starting to get feeling back to hands and face. Her stomach still writhed, complaining it was empty and yet daring her to put anything in it at the same time.

She rubbed a towel across herself haphazardly and pulled her clothes back on, wincing as the fabric dragged along the wet skin. Once dressed, she staggered back to bed, pulling all of the covers up around her face, snuggling deep into the depths of the sheets.

As she nodded off, she reaffirmed her decisions in the shower. No more emotions. She was a blank page; whatever Rob wanted, that's what she would present. She wouldn't open up to anyone any more.

"Shhh, enough of that," a calming voice whispered. "You've had enough hurt. Go to sleep."

Her eyes sank closed.

"That's right. Sleep. Go to sleep, little one," it spoke gently.

Samantha faded away.

Chapter Seventeen

I sat up, my head ringing. I looked around at the dusty pianos that surrounded me. My fingers picked at the worn wooden floor, and I called out to see if anyone was around. There was no answer.

I stood up, wobbling from pain, and walked over to the window, as it was the sole source of lighting at the moment. The cat sat at the piano as he always had, a thick layer of dust coating his fur. Outside, the sky was an orange-red. The trees were shaking to and fro, and lightning flashed among the clouds. I moved on to the door and turned the deadbolt. The door creaked open, ringing the faded bell that hung above it.

I peeked my head out, but saw nobody on the street. The blue bicycle I had ridden before lay in front of me, its tires and seat slashed and its frame bent. I knelt and picked up the chain that sat next to it. It was locked tight with rust and had come apart in several places. I set it back down and wiped the orange residue off on my jeans.

As I stood up, a motion down the street caught my eye. It was the little white mouse. It stared at me with a disinterested expression. It began to clean its whiskers, never breaking eye contact. As I glared back, a small hand lifted it up. The little girl with the large panic eyes held him close to her stomach and petted the top of his head. She looked up at me, blonde bangs falling into her eyes, and turned her head to the side.

I gingerly began to approach her. She didn't move or make a sound but looked at me through the side of her wide black and red eyes. I felt like she could see into my soul, her gaze was so intense. I had almost reached her, when I heard footsteps behind me.

"Don't go any closer!" a voice commanded.

I turned and saw Thomas, umbrella closed and clutched in one hand, the other pointing at me.

"Why not?" I asked. "We're fine."

"It's not fine, look at her eyes," he replied. "You need to back away now!"
I looked back at her. She hadn't moved, still clutching the mouse to her, but she was now staring at Thomas and trembling. A single tear rolled out from one eye.

I shook my head. "No, I need to figure this out."

She peered up at me and raised her arm, wordlessly asking me to hold her hand.

I moved to take her hand in mine, but immediately heard howling and laughing coming around the corner. I looked up in time to see a crowd of people with panic eyes step out onto the street. They lurched towards me, cackling and screeching.

Thomas grabbed my arm and yanked me towards him. He opened the umbrella up and swirled it around us. When he lifted it back up and closed it, we were standing in the room with the piano.

I slammed my fists into his chest, knocking him off balance.

"Why did you do that?"

"You were in danger!" he replied. "I had to get you out of there!"

"How will I figure out what's happening if I can't get close?" I demanded.

He threw open his arms and dramatically shrugged.

"Maybe you're not supposed to figure it out," he stated bluntly.

I screamed in frustration and kicked a pile of papers that sat near the window.

"I'm leaving. I'm going back down there," I declared and threw a leg over the ledge.

He grabbed my arm again and jerked me into the room.

"No," he yelled, "you aren't going anywhere!"

I shoved him, and he stumbled backwards into the wall. A hole opened up behind him. Through it, I could see filing cabinets, books, papers, all sitting in the dark.

"What is that?" I asked.

"Nothing you need to worry about," he said, dusting himself off.

"What is it?" I asked again.

"Nothing," he repeated.

"Did you wall up this room to keep it from me?" I asked incredulously.

"It's nothing you need to worry about," he said again.

I stared at him with a horrified expression. "What are you keeping from me?"

Thomas looked at me and sighed. "If you had any idea, you would fall apart."

"That's not for you to decide," I told him. "That's for me to figure out."

He shook his head. "It would affect more than just you."

"Who? Who else would it affect? Rob? Because I think we can rule that one out," I said.

He gave me a strange look, almost one of confusion. "No, not Rob."

"Then who?" I cried.

He shook his head again and sat down at the piano, still facing me.

"Just trust me when I tell you that I can't have you put in danger."

"Why should I trust you?" I asked. "Because you say I should?"

"Precisely," he replied.

"Who are you?" I demanded. "I don't even know who you are!"

He hung his head. "You know who I am," he said softly.

"No, I don't," I asserted. "You're just a guy who keeps things from me, and keeps whisking me away to this godforsaken room. You're just some asshole who refuses to tell me what's going on!"

"I'm with you every single day!" he shouted back.

I blinked. That didn't make sense. I had only seen him in a few of my dreams.

"I make sure you eat when you don't feel like it. I make sure you get to all of your damn appointments. I keep you supplied with everything you need to go about your day," he spilled forth. "I keep you clean and healthy and functioning, and I keep this whole damn place going like clockwork!"

I was confused. I shook my head.

"I tell Charity to shut the fuck up when she's being awful," he continued. "I tell Eric to lay off when he's being too much. I call off Ariana when she's ready to blow. Hell, I even tell Laura to go check on you when things get rough."

My mouth gaped open. Who was Laura?

"I keep quiet those who need to be kept quiet," he said in a low voice. "I let out those who need to be let out and keep in those who don't. I oversee everything that goes in and out. Period. And you dare ask me who I am?"

He stood up and grabbed my shirt. He leaned in close to my face.

"I am your fucking gatekeeper," he hissed.

I blinked again.

He stepped away and sat back down at the piano. He began to pick at the keys, playing a small, lilting tune.

I staggered back to the windowsill and leaned on it, taken aback by this sudden turn of events. I had never doubted that he held an important role in everything but to wield this much power? There had been a voice all those years chiding me, prodding me to do better. Was that really him all along?

I adjusted my weight, and the piano briefly stopped playing.

"I'm not leaving," I quietly assured him. The playing resumed.

I peered again at the hole in the wall. The files beyond it taunted me. Could they contain information about the panic eyes, the little girl, even the mouse? Could they help me with my real life problems? I had vague memories of being in that file room once before, but the recollection of what had ensued was foggy.

"How do I proceed?" I finally asked aloud.

"With what?" Thomas replied, continuing to play.

"Everything," I responded. "I still need to know."

"You think if you figure it out, you can defeat it," he said.

I nodded. "If I can defeat it, then I won't have the same nightmares over and over again," I postulated.

Thomas gave a rueful chuckle.

"What?" I asked. "What's so funny?"

"Your naivety," he said. "There isn't always an end to things."

"Says who?"

He took a deep breath. "Says a room full of files."

"So that's an excuse not to try?" I sputtered.

"Your safety is an excuse not to try."

"I'm not safe while the panic eyes are still a thing."

"But what's guaranteeing that your digging around will bring an end to them?"

"So, I shouldn't even-"

I stopped and shook my head.

"We're going in circles. You can't hold me here forever. I have a right to know why this is happening, and I feel like that little girl can give me that information."

Thomas pulled his hands away from the keys and turned to look at me. His face was more pallid than usual and was shadowed in exhaustion.

"This whole scenario, it's like a horror movie, right?" he asked.

I reluctantly nodded.

"When, in a horror movie, have you ever rooted for the characters to go towards the little kid with the creepy eyes?"

I swallowed and glared at him. He stared back, unblinking.

"What are you getting at?" I asked.

"Little girls aren't always a sign of good. Sometimes they reflect the darker, more twisted shadows around them."

I shook my head.

"She seems so innocent," I said.

"They all are," he replied. "I wasn't speaking of her directly, but what she represents. Sometimes the worst things you can imagine are tied to the appearance of children. This plague, these panic eyes, there is a connection to her; I will agree with you on that. What I cannot do is condone putting yourself at risk to figure it out, particularly when it may change nothing."

I frowned at him, my breath hissing out through my nose. He rolled his eyes.

"We don't even know if she can speak," he pleaded.

"And we won't ever know if we don't try," I argued.

He grimaced and shook his head. "No. Absolutely not. I'm not even going to humor this conversation further."

His hand fluttered at me as he turned back around.

"You can wake up now," he said.

I opened my mouth to argue, but he interrupted.

"I'm not going to do it for you, but you need to wake up now."

I did feel shaky, sort of threadbare like an illusion.

"This isn't over," I said defiantly.

He sighed and began to play a mournful tune.

"It never is."

Chapter Eighteen

Samantha woke up just in time to throw up what little acid her stomach had produced. She clutched the trash can like it was her best friend in her time of need. The smell that arose from it would argue otherwise.

As if mocking her, her stomach growled loudly. She groaned and rubbed her belly, letting her forehead rest on the side of the can. She knew she needed to drink some water at the very least, but surely it couldn't hurt to have a little bread or something, too? She reluctantly pulled away from the bin, grabbed her phone, and shuffled to the door. She peeked her head around the frame and peered down into the living room. There were no sounds; the house seemed to be empty.

Gingerly, she made her way down the stairs, clutching the railing for balance. She was a little dizzy still, and her stomach growled and writhed. She wondered briefly if she was still drunk and tightened her grip on the banister.

As her foot hit the living room floor, she swiveled her head around wildly, searching for any sign of Rob. The only thing she found was a stack of pillows and a folded blanket on the couch. She sighed sadly. She had really screwed things up. She grabbed the blanket, smelling it deeply first, then flinging it around her hunched form. She made her way into the kitchen, where she was surprised to find a brown bag sitting on the counter.

Inside sat a delicious looking poppy seed bagel, with egg and cheese oozing out the sides. She looked for a note or a receipt, then checked her phone. She did have a text message.

Her fingers shook as she opened it up. It was from Rob.

"Left you breakfast in the kitchen. Drink lots of water."

She smiled and texted him back.

"Thank you! I love you!"

She stared at her phone and the word "delivered" for a few minutes. When nothing changed, she set it down and poured herself a glass of water.

Like a greedy little gnome, she cloaked herself in the blanked, settled the water in the crook of her arm, and clutched the bag and phone in either hand. She shuffled into the living room and sat down, turning the tv on and flipping the channel to cartoons.

As she ate the bagel, she nervously kept glancing at her phone. Eventually, when she was almost finished, she saw the message change to "read". She picked it up and stared, willing a new message from Rob to appear. None did.

She sighed. The bagel had satisfied her, but now she wasn't sure what to do. She still felt a bit queasy, and she knew she couldn't show her face at the convention. Rob's words echoed in her head.

"You need to see a fucking therapist."

She opened up a browser on her phone and searched "therapist" with her zip code. Tons of results came up, and she started to scroll.

"Ugh, religious guidance? No thanks," a voice said disgustedly.

"Ooh, that one does touch stuff. That could be interesting," another remarked.

"What about the techie one? They probably have some crazy sci-fi technology they could use to fix everything!" one declared excitedly.

As she scrolled through, the voices continued to swirl around. She was in over her head. There were so many therapists offering a million different approaches, Samantha had no idea where to begin.

"Well, what's wrong with you?" a voice asked pointedly.

"I hear you guys," she replied out loud. "That's a pretty good start."

"You can't tell anyone," another voice hissed. "They'll send you away like your brother. You wouldn't like that."

Samantha shivered as a chill fell over her. Her brother had been sent to a facility a few years ago, for many of the same things she herself went through. She had been as supportive as she could be towards her family, but it was a period of time that haunted her. Having to see her own baby brother have to face that challenge, knowing that her parents and other brother were so far away from him, that she herself was away at school, it broke her heart. On a more selfish level, she swore never to be sent anywhere. There would be no grippy socks for Samantha, no overnight watches. Sure, she heard voices and even had a suicidal thought or two, but overall, there was nothing wrong with her. She was heavily depressed and wracked with anxiety, but who wasn't? That had to be more of a generational problem than a personal one.

Generational or not, she figured that "depression" and "anxiety" would be good keywords. She typed in the keywords and submitted the search. The results barely changed.

Samantha groaned and put her phone down. The room was starting to spin again. She pulled her legs up onto the couch, curled up on her side, and tugged the blanket up over her head.

Rob had made himself clear, and Samantha felt immensely guilty for everything that had happened. If she didn't find a therapist, would he leave? It would serve her right, she concluded. She had to strike that delicate balance between seeking help and not seeming broken, showing him the work without making it seem like work. She needed to fix things while carrying herself with confidence. The best way to pull this off was to start putting things in place while she was alone. She slipped an arm out and patted around on the coffee table until her hand landed on her phone. She pulled it back under the blanket and turned the screen on.

There were no messages.

She opened the search again and pressed on. Most therapists in her area had religious ties, something she was adamantly against. She had her fill of religion when she was younger; if it didn't cure her then, it certainly wouldn't now. She noted that the ones who were specifically non-religious directly advertised their work with the queer community. She thought it noble of them, but given that she was comfortable with her bisexuality, she skipped over those listings as well.

"You're not going to find an ad for a therapist seeking you specifically," a voice commented.

"It needs to be a good fit," she asserted.

Rather than narrowing her search down in a constructive way, she started to eliminate options for frivolous reasons: too young, too old, too masculine, too feminine, their office was on the other side of town, their office was too close. She scrolled through the listings quickly, her heart rate speeding up.

"You're never going to find one at this rate," a voice complained.

"You're never going to find one," another repeated mockingly. "You're never going to find one. You're never going to find one."

"If you don't find one," yet another voiced desperately, "then Rob will leave you, and you will be alone. Nobody will ever want to be with you. You'll be broken forever. You'll be alone. Nobody will want you. Rob will leave. You have to find one, you have to!"

Samantha cried out in frustration and shut her phone off again, tossing it back onto the table. Her breathing became more rapid and shallow, and her eyes welled up with tears. She pulled her knees to her chest and panted. Her feet shook back and forth, and her fingers curled and uncurled nervously.

She couldn't be alone. She had sworn the night before that she would no longer open up to people, but she still needed them to want her in their lives, especially Rob. The thought of everyone hating her made her stomach sink. There had to be a middle ground.

"What if you got a therapist and just didn't tell them much?" a calm voice suggested.

Samantha's movements stilled.

"Just let them scrape the surface of the depression and anxiety, just enough to let them feel like they're doing something, but not enough to get sent away," it continued. "Then Rob will be happy, and you won't have to really have to have your head trounced through."

Samantha slowly nodded.

"And since you won't really be using their services," it said, "you don't have to narrow your search down. Just pick one, go to a few sessions, tell Rob you're cured, and never worry about it again."

Could it be that easy?

"I think he's just looking for a little effort," another voice chimed in. "He wants to see something take place after what happened, and as long as it looks like you're trying, you're golden!"

Samantha sat up, gathering the blanket onto her lap. This plan could work.

"Now, you also need to make a game plan, show him you're really determined to be your best."

She knew exactly what the voice was saying. She checked her phone again. There were no messages. She set the blanket aside and climbed up the stairs, feeling her head spin a bit with each step. She went to her backpack and rifled through it until she found the notebook she had bought and a pen. She brought them downstairs, setting them on the table, and finished her glass of water. It made her stomach churn, but she dutifully refilled it at the kitchen sink.

As a brightly colored, highly energetic cartoon played in the background, Samantha put on her focus face and began to write. She made a list of all the things she needed to do to be a better person. She audaciously wrote "therapy" in large block letters at the top of it, knowing she would leave this open on the table for Rob to find later. She included things like "go running everyday", "study for the GRE", and "start streaming art". She thought about Rob's perfect partner, the women she had found in that folder once upon a time, and added "do hair and makeup everyday". She had gotten complacent, truthfully, and it really couldn't be that attractive. She considered adding "dye hair" to the list but decided to hold off. That would be laying it on a little too thick.

She carefully placed the notebook on the table at an angle, with the pen laying in the crease of the open pages, as if she had tossed it down after writing. She drank most of the water in the glass and set it next to the book, then bunched the blanket up at the end of the couch, completing the look. This should be enough to fool Rob.

"And if he asks how you're doing?"

"I'm fine," Samantha said.

"No, not quite."

"I'm feeling great," she corrected. "That was an awful night, and I'm sorry, but now I realize what I have to do, and I'm feeling so motivated!"

"There we go," the voice commended.

She couldn't tell Rob how she really felt. She was still panicky and very depressed. Her embarrassment from the night before would prevent her from being social for a very long time. Having a plan did make her feel a bit better, though. She had a script; she just needed to put on the mask.

Her limbs were starting to ache, and her stomach was feeling queasy again. She nodded quietly to herself and climbed the stairs again.

She put her backpack back in order and started up the shower. She reluctantly looked in the mirror. Her hair was matted and sticking up on one side, and her eyes were bloodshot. A crust of drool had formed on her chin. Her skin was pallid and a slight green color. She shivered and stepped into the warm water, letting it envelop her. She scrubbed everywhere she could reach, not stepping out until her skin was red and her hair squeaked between her fingers.

She wrapped herself in a towel and dried her hair. She carefully parted it in the middle and braided the sides back, letting the rest of her hair tumble down in curls. Feeling dizzy, she grabbed her makeup bag and sat at the edge of the bed. She used the mirror in her compact as a guide and made up her full face.

She put everything back in the bag and set it aside, feeling her head spin again. She stumbled over to her suitcase and pulled some clothes out. She wrestled everything on, feeling weaker and weaker as she went. Finally, with shorts and tank top on, she tripped back to the bed and laid down. She stared at the ceiling, feeling the bed sway a little to each side. Her eyelids grew heavy and a sort of weight gathered in her limbs.

As her mind faded, she heard her phone buzz.

Chapter Nineteen

A persistent buzzing noise caught my attention. I opened my eyes and looked around the room.

Everyone had their noses buried in their books, as the teacher sat at her desk grading. Haunting posters of eyes and thin, sickly looking people hung on the walls. The words "turn it off" were written in large block letters on the chalkboard. My own book lay open in front of me, but the words kept blurring together. The thin strands of light coming in through the windows only made it that much more difficult to read. There were no lights hanging from the impossibly tall, looming ceiling, and no lamps on the desks. Even the hallway looked dim through the doorway.

The buzzing started up again, and I felt myself become detached and lightheaded. My eyes darted around, desperately trying to find the source. They settled on Charity, sitting in the back of the classroom. She met my gaze and slowly lifted a finger to her lips. I nodded, and she pointed to the clock at the front of the classroom. I turned and watched the minute hand jerk towards the twelve in time with the buzzing.

As soon as the time read three, everyone began to put their books away in strange, silent synchronicity. There was no alarm, and nobody had been looking up from the thick, yellowing pages. Still, they acted as if a signal had been given. I joined them, closing my book and sliding it into my red, beat up backpack. When I looked back up, they were all staring at me. Even the teacher had stood up and glared at me, hunched over her desk, hands carefully poised into claws over the dark wood. The posters had grown in size, peeling at the corners away from the walls, silently watching.

Charity walked past me, bag slung over her shoulder.

"Get up," she whispered between gritted teeth.

I swallowed and grabbed my backpack, carefully standing. I turned around and backed out of the classroom, staring back at the sea of eyes following me.

Once I had made it into the hallway, I picked up the pace. I needed to find my locker so I could swap my books out. Unfortunately, both sides of the hall were lined with lockers, the numbers faded to the point of illegibility, not that I could remember my locker number anyway. People began to swarm around and the sound of lockers opening and slamming shut filled the hallway. Nobody spoke.

I wandered up and down, waiting for some sort of familiarity to click into place. One spot seemed right, but the padlock on the latch proved to be yet another obstacle. I began to panic, fearing what would happen if I could not get the right books to take home. If I didn't get the right ones, I wouldn't be able to do the homework, and I would fail all the tests. I couldn't be a failure; I absolutely could not.

I twisted and turned the dial over and over again, begging for something to work. Eventually, it popped open, and the door swung out. I was in tears as I pulled textbook after textbook off the shelves and placed them into my bag. Eventually, the bag was full, but there were still more textbooks. The panic began to set in again, so I desperately scoured the spines looking for the subjects.

Chemistry I definitely needed to take; the same could be said of algebra. Did I have history homework? I couldn't remember. I kept it just in case. Then, I picked up a Latin book.

This wasn't right, I thought. I didn't take Latin until college.

College.

I had already graduated college.

If I had already graduated college, then why was I in high school?

A wind whipped through the hallway, scattering papers and slamming locker doors. As the floor began to writhe, I closed my own locker and shouldered my backpack. Clearly, this was some sort of remedial thing.

The wind died down.

I walked down the hallway, turning right to cut through the lobby, past the vending machines and small farmers market booths. A newspaper stand had some freshly baked cinnamon rolls on its counter, but I ignored it. Just past it, I could see the buses outside.

I climbed a short flight of stairs and had just reached the giant glass doors, when the buses started to roll away. I flung the doors open and ran to my bus. The driver ignored my cries and arm waving, driving off down the road. As I watched the tail lights fade in the distance, I fumbled for the phone in my pocket.

I tried both my parents, but there was no answer. I was a bit relieved, to be honest, as I knew they would be mad that I had missed my bus. I tried my aunt next. She picked up, but there was only garbled nonsense on the other end of the line. I tried to get her to repeat herself or to speak clearly, but the call dropped. I sighed. It looked like I was walking.

I started to trod off down the sidewalk, not looking forward to the long, highway-adjacent walk I had before me.

"You know, it's pretty dangerous to walk alone like this," a voice chimed in next to me.

Charity had appeared at my side, chewing on the end of a curly lock, regarding me cooly.

I shrugged. "I don't have a choice," I said. "I've tried calling."

She wrinkled her nose. "Phones don't really work here," she replied.

"I gathered," I said, nodding.

We walked in silence for a bit.

"You really think you can just change?" she finally asked.

I raised my eyebrow. "How do you mean?" I asked.

She looked at me, eyes narrowing.

"Nothing," she slowly said. "Forget I said it."

Everything was silent again.

Eventually the small town turned into overgrown fields. Every once in a while a motorcycle or a truck would pass by. We carefully stepped over piles of boxes and clothes as they came up.

"You know, I'm only trying to help," she started.

"Help with what?" I asked.

"Everything," she replied. "I don't hate you, not really. You just need to know the truth in order to change and grow."

"Like what?"

She rolled her eyes. "Like, you're fat, for one. Lay off the carbs."

I frowned and looked down. I had a little bit of a pudge, but you could still see my hips clearly defined.

"No, not here," she clarified. "Out there."

I nodded slowly, hoping she would clarify. She didn't.

"You also need to quit being a snivelling cry baby. That scene in the hallway? It's a freaking locker. You didn't even need those books anyway."

"Could've told me sooner," I scoffed.

She stared at me incredulously. "There really is a disconnect, isn't there? How long did it take you to realize you weren't in high school anymore?"

"I had to be there for a reason," I replied.

"Did Eric have this much trouble getting through to you?" she asked.

"No, but I'm much better at communication than you are," a chipper voice piped up.

We turned and saw Eric taking loping steps towards us.

"Good afternoon, ladies!" he said with a grin.

Charity rolled her eyes again.

"Mind if I join you on this stroll?" he asked.

I smiled and waved him in. I now walked with them on either side of me.

"Some instances are a little thicker than others," he told Charity. "You just have to assess and roll accordingly."

He looked at me. "How was school?"

I shuddered. "It was quiet, and there were eyes everywhere."

He nodded. "Good thing we're heading home, then."

I nodded back. "Yep, home."

Slowly, a heaviness began to settle in my mind, similar to the feeling I had when I remembered graduating college.

"Wait," I said slowly. "Home to my parents? Or home to the apartment?"

Eric stared at me expectantly.

"Parents or apartment?" I repeated.

"Which do you think?" Charity asked.

I paused.

"Is this a-"

"Now now," Eric interrupted, "no time for that. See, Charity, that's all you got to do."

I remembered some of what had been happening. Rob was mad at me. Cassie was upset. I had no friends.

"Oh no," I mumbled, tears welling up in my eyes.

"Not again," Charity groaned. "Get a hold of yourself!"

"I think you're doing great," Eric cheered me on.

"I have to find the problem," I said. "I have to find the root."

Eric laughed. "Hoo boy, that's a tall order."

I glared at him. "How can I fix it if I don't?"

He smiled. "I didn't say you were wrong," he replied. "It's just not that simple."

We walked for a time while I mulled it over. Charity and Eric began to bicker back and forth, him smirking, and her growing redder and redder.

I began to think about Thomas and the tower, the file room, and how it had been sealed off. Maybe that is where I needed to look.

"Take me to the file room," I finally said aloud.

They both stopped arguing and looked at me. I reached down and picked up a basketball that had rolled over to my feet.

"Well?" I asked, dribbling the ball a bit.

Eric shook his head. "No," he said quietly.

Charity nodded. "We can't do that," she retorted.

I shot the ball into the field, watching as a scattering of butterflies flew away in its wake.

"Why not?"

Eric frowned, an expression that seemed unnatural on his face.

"That's not our area to explore."

"You aren't allowed?" I asked cagily.

"You're not allowed," Charity shot back.

"Says who?" I persisted.

"Says everyone," Eric responded. "It's just not done."

"Why not?" I asked.

They both glared at me.

"If I can get to the file room," I continued, "I think I'll be able to pinpoint where to start."

"The files aren't for you," Eric replied quietly.

"If they're not for me, then who are they for?" I demanded.

"Do you think this is all about you?" Charity asked.

"Is it not?" I cried out.

"No!" she shouted. "It's not! Quit being a self absorbed baby! Look outside yourself!"

"No!" I shouted back. "I'm tired of looking out for everyone but myself!"

"Oh yeah, you definitely had a great start to that," she replied snarkily.

My mouth gaped open.

"You took that experience, and made it about you," she said. "You hurt so many people, made so many uncomfortable, and your reaction was what?"

She pitched her voice up into a squeaky whine.

"Oh, I must be alone now. Oh, I'll never be myself again. Oh, what will Rob think? Oh, I must make myself over to be perfect in his eyes. I, me, my, myself, I, me, mine."

She glared at me. "It's always about you."

Eric put a hand on her shoulder.

"That's enough," he said.

I took a deep breath.

"I'm going to that file room, with or without your help."

I stormed off down the sidewalk. They ran after me.

"Don't do this," Eric pleaded. "It won't turn out well."

"At the very least, Thomas is going to go ballistic," Charity added.

I waved it off.

"What do you need from us?" Eric asked. "What can we do to help?"

"Get me into the file room," I said.

"Aside from that," he replied.

I turned to him.

"You know, I would expect her to not want to help," I said, pointing at Charity, "but you? I thought I could count on you."

His face fell. Charity stared blankly. I turned around and kept walking.

Eventually, the fields turned into a large dirt and gravel road. I turned down it, avoiding the large sinkhole to the side. A snake crossed my path, and I shuffled backwards, awkwardly bumping into someone.

"Are you still following me?" I asked, spinning around.

It wasn't Eric or Charity.

A large shadowy figure loomed over me, with swirling black and red eyes. It had no other features. A feeling of dread swept over me. I scrambled back, trying to get away, only to slip and fall onto the snake. It whipped around and bit my leg, sinking its fangs in just below my knee.

I screamed in pain, grabbing the serpent and casting it off to the side. I shuffled backwards as blood trailed down my leg.

The shadow took a deep breath and the sky darkened. Its panic eyes swirled maddeningly. It raised an arm, and I heard howling and laughing in the distance.

I shakily stood up and began to limp away, but the shadow followed, growing larger and larger. It opened a mouth, one that had not been there before, and bellowed out a long howl.

Rain started to fall. My shoe was full of blood and my leg burned. A hand grabbed my shoulder and yanked me back.

Ariana placed herself between me and the monster. Eric swooped in, scooping me up under my arms, letting me use him as a crutch.

Ariana turned and yelled at us.

"Go!"

Eric helped me run. The howling and the laughter grew louder, and my leg felt like it was on fire. We ran as fast as we could.

Eventually, we came to a large apple tree, hunched over a faded driveway that led to a dilapidated house.

Eric maneuvered me underneath the branches.

"Alright, it's your favorite part," he muttered.

"I'm sorry," I said, crying. "I'm sorry. I didn't mean it. I know you're my friend."

He smiled.

"No worries, darling. I know. We need to get you out, though."

I shook my head from side to side.

"No, it hurts, I can't run any more."

He smoothed the hair away from my face.

"You don't have to. Just wake up."

I blinked at him.

"Wake up," he repeated.

I nodded and scrunched my face up.

"Wake up," I said. "Wake up."

I opened my eyes. Eric was still there, and I could see the shadowy figure coming down the road. He looked angry, waving his arms in the air while howling with that gaping maw.

In the fields, a number of people were running towards him, darting around in a mad frenzy, all of them screaming and laughing.

I closed my eyes again. "Wake. Up."

I opened them. He was even closer. My leg throbbed, and I was getting dizzy. My stomach was in knots.

I closed my eyes. "Wake! Up!"

Chapter Twenty

Samantha scrambled out of bed and fell to the floor. She frantically wheeled her legs until her back hit the wall. Her breathing was shallow and erratic. The monster had never been fully realized before. Was she going too far? Pushing too hard?

With a start, she realized that Ariana had not been on the road when she looked up.

"I'm fine," a voice spoke up. "Don't ever worry about me."

Samantha nodded and shakily stood up. She tried to swallow but found her mouth was bone dry. She smoothed her hair down and tugged at her shorts. By pulling herself together, she was able to stabilize mentally.

She picked up her phone and saw a missed call from Rob. He hadn't left a voicemail or a text, and it had been hours ago. She hesitated a moment, then called him back.

The phone rang four times before he answered.

"Yeah?"

"I missed your call," she said in an inquisitive, hopeful tone.

"Were you asleep?" he asked pointedly.

Samantha's face reddened. "Yeah, I needed a nap."

He didn't say anything. Samantha could hear people laughing and talking in the background.

"So, where are you at?" she asked with a chipper note in her voice.

"Out," he replied.

Samantha bit her lip and nodded. This conversation wasn't getting anywhere.

"Look, why did you call me?" she asked.

"What did you want for dinner?" he responded.

"I'm up for whatever!" she said excitedly. "When did you want to come get me? Or did you want me to meet you?"

"I figured I would grab you something on my way back from this."

Samantha blinked. "Oh. You're at dinner already?"

"Yeah, some people wanted to hang out."

The questions flared up in her, and the voices began to swirl with accusations.

"Ah, that's nice," she said in a low voice. "Who all's there?"

There was another pause on the line. A girl's laugh echoed through the phone.

"What do you want for dinner, Sam?"

Her lower lip trembled. "Surprise me," she said bluntly and hung the phone up.

She tossed it on the bed and paced around. A quick peek in the mirror showed that her hair and makeup had stayed fairly intact through her nap.

"Might as well tear it all apart," a voice hissed. "He won't care. He hates you."

"If he hated you, he wouldn't be bringing you food," another reassured her.

"He feels obligated. You're an obligation. You're a burden," yet another taunted.

She did some touch ups and paced again before snatching her phone up.

She got on social media, pulling up his profile. He had been getting tagged in photos all day. The latest one was him at a big wooden table, giving the camera a big, open mouth grin with both thumbs raised up high. Jason and Todd peered out from the end of the table, toasting each other with giant steins of beer. Across from Rob was Cassie, hair in two French braids, and wearing a tiny sundress. She looked like a model fresh out of a magazine. She was blowing a kiss to the camera. Everyone else was behaving similarly, most of whom Samantha didn't recognize.

She began to scroll through the images. Most were him with middle aged men, his average audience demographic. Samantha smiled at all the goofy grins. She was sure Rob was tickled that so many people were recognizing him and asking for pictures.

She scrolled down and the next picture melted the smile off her face. It was Rob, sparkling green eyes crinkled and mouth open in mid laugh. Cassie had her arms wrapped around his chest and her head on his shoulder, also laughing. His hands held a plush video game character up in the air triumphantly.

Cassie had been the one to post it and declared in the caption that, "Robket is simply the best. Fight me."

Samantha took a deep breath.

"You'd win," a voice said reassuringly. "You know, if you fought."

"Not now," she said through gritted teeth.

The next few pictures were also of them goofing around. Standing back to back with serious faces, her on his back with her arms and legs spread out like a starfish while he looped his arms under her thighs, and the two of them trying on vr headsets together.

Samantha went back to her homepage and looked through some other people's posts. It seemed like everyone was having fun. She swallowed her pride and sent messages to Jason and Todd, apologizing for her behavior the night before. She pulled up Cassie's profile and hesitated. Apologizing to them was one thing, but her?

She shook her head and closed the page. Curious, she looked at the next day's schedule for the convention. It was the last day and ended early, but there were a few interesting panels. It would also be the day that the booths would have things marked down. She could grab a few last minute things, maybe even pick up something for Rob to try to make up. She knew there were going to be a few parties, and it would be a good time for her to put on her mask and become the Samantha Rob would want.

Her phone buzzed as Jason messaged her back.

It was a selfie of him and Todd.

"We're cool," he said. "Thank you for the apology. We now know your kryptonite!"

"Haha, good," she replied. "Yes, keep me away from that stuff!"

Jason sent her a wink back.

She thought for a moment, then typed in, "Is Rob still with you guys?"

The message flipped to read, but the phone stayed quiet. Samantha stared anxiously at the screen, but it didn't change. She sighed and went back to the schedule. There was a panel on being in a relationship with an influencer. She added it to her calendar, along with one about horror games.

A message from Jason popped up. Her fingers shook as she opened it.

"He left a little while ago. He told Barry he had to run an errand and that he would be at the purple party after that. Are you going to be there? He said you were sleeping and wasn't sure when you'd be up."

Samantha pondered for a bit.

"Yeah, I'll be there! See you then?"

"See you then!"

Samantha looked down at her black tank and her jean shorts. There was nothing purple there. She then remembered the purple hair gel and smiled. She dug the tube out from the bottom of the suitcase. She undid her braids and painted the middle strand purple before braiding them back. She then added a touch of purple to the ends of her curls.

She had just set the tube down when she heard the front door open. She frantically smoothed her hair again and poked at her face, willing the makeup to look good. She waited a minute before going downstairs, giving Rob time to find her notebook.

Fortunately, he was standing next to the coffee table when she arrived. He held out a white styrofoam box to her.

"What did you get me?" she asked

"Chicken and steamed vegetables," he replied. "I wasn't sure if your stomach could handle anything else."

"Thank you," she said and took it from him.

She curled up on one end of the couch, away from the book. Rob went into the kitchen and brought back a fork. As she ate, he went upstairs and showered. When he came back down, she was nearly done. He had on a dark purple button up with a black vest and a galaxy patterned tie.

"Ooh, I'll be done in a minute," she said.

He paused halfway through putting his shoes on.

"Sorry?" he replied.

Samantha held up a forkful of chicken. "I'm almost done," she said. "Then we can head out."

Rob stared at her. "No," he said finally.

Samantha took a deep breath.

"Look, Rob, I'm sorry," she said. "I screwed up, I really did, but I intend to make up for it. I've already apologized to Jason and Todd. I won't have a drop to drink. I will happily apologize to anyone else you want, or I'll talk to no one, whichever you prefer. Please, just let me join you. Let me be your date."

Rob looked at her sadly. "This is a very important party," he said.

"I know."

"All the larger streamers are going to be there."

"Crystal clear."

"It's an open bar."

"Not a drop, I swear."

He sighed.

"Okay," he said. "But it's going to be a lot of shop. I don't know if you'll be into that."

"That's perfect!" Samantha exclaimed. "I'm planning on starting the channel up. See?"

She pointed at the book, watching Rob's eyes fall onto it. As he read the page, she smiled to herself. This plan could absolutely work.

He nodded. "Okay," he said again, this time a little more confidently.

Samantha clapped excitedly and finished her food. Truth be told, her stomach was rather upset, but she squashed that feeling down and ignored it. She couldn't figure out if it was from the food or the prospect of being her "new" self in a crowd of people.

She set the box down on the table and jumped up.

"Let's go!" she exclaimed.

Rob swallowed and nodded. He arranged for a ride share to pick them up.

As they waited, she reached up and brushed her hand through his hair.

"You're so handsome," she said. "I'm so lucky."

He nodded, rather than sharing the sentiment as he usually did.

Samantha's face fell.

"I'm really sorry, Rob. If you don't want me to come with you to this thing, I understand."

"You're fine," he replied, leaving it at that.

Samantha sighed and peered down the road, looking for the car.

Once it arrived, she crawled into the back seat, expecting Rob to get in next to her. Instead, he rode up front.

He and the driver struck up a conversation about gaming, and Samantha stared out the window. She felt isolated, but she had also accounted for that. How else would you feel if you stopped letting people in? She would have to be the introvert with an extrovert mask for this to work, and that would be a rather isolating experience. She would essentially be removing herself from the equation and leaving only the physical husk to do the work.

The car stopped outside of the club, and they stepped out. She reached for Rob's hand, but he stepped ahead of her.

"Brian!" he shouted.

The tall man in a trucker hat turned. "Rob!" he called back.

They hugged, and Brian craned his neck to see Samantha. She smiled at him, recognizing him from social media and Rob's streams. She stepped forward to meet him.

"You must be Sam," he said, disengaging from Rob.

She nodded and opened her mouth to introduce herself, but he interrupted.

"Well, where's the pizza?" he asked in a shrill voice. "You were supposed to bring the pizza!"

He and Rob laughed, partaking in some inside joke, but Samantha did not. She suddenly felt very small. Her breath caught in her throat and her head began to ache.

"I, um, I-"

"Oh, come on Sam, get with the program!" he said, then laughed again.

He and Rob then started to talk about their streams. They wandered over to the bar, where Rob grabbed a beer, then went to stand near a pillar. Samantha followed at a distance, trying to keep her breathing slow and regular. All the purple in the room began to swirl together. A girl bumped into her, spilling her drink on Samantha. The girl sneered at her. "Excuse you," she said and moved on.

Samantha went up to the bar and asked for some napkins. As she blotted the moisture from her tank top, she heard a familiar voice.

"Vodka tonic, light on the tonic."

She craned her next to see two cherry red braids hanging down over the bar. Cassie's face was illuminated by her phone. She had changed from her sundress into a dark purple bodycon dress with wide cutouts around the waist. The bartender slid her the glass with a sideways glance. Cassie ignored him and took a swig, eyes trained on the small screen.

Samantha careened away from the bar and made a beeline for the pillar Rob was at. She stopped just a few feet away, worried about her next interaction with Brian.

She started to panic.

She pushed and shoved her way through the crowd until she reached a patio. A few smokers milled around there, but she didn't mind pulling the secondhand smoke through her lungs if it meant she was away from all the people. She closed her eyes and envisioned her extrovert mask going back on. She started to get a weird floating feeling in the back of her head, like a current was pulling at her. She let her mind float on it.

As she walked back into the room, she watched herself. It was like playing a game in third person.

Brian called out to her, "Hey, pizza girl!"

She felt the movement in her throat, heard the voice, but did not recognize it.

"What up, lanky legs?!"

Brian blinked, and Rob turned his head to stare at Samantha.

Samantha watched as her body walked over to them and slung an arm around Rob.

"I hear you're going to be streaming soon," Brian said slowly, eyeing her curiously.

"Yeah, just a little something fun," her voice replied.

She felt another shift, another current tugging at her.

"Why?" her voice asked. "You gonna watch?"

She leaned forward and winked, still with an arm around Rob.

Brian's eyebrows raised. "I guess I will."

She grinned. "Good. See you there!"

She turned and walked over to the bar and ordered pineapple juice with a cherry in it. She sipped on it as she surveyed the crowd. Samantha could barely register the taste. She was feeling foggier and foggier. She closed her eyes and opened them to the bathroom mirror.

She blinked and thought about how she had gotten there. She vaguely remembered talking to a group of guys at one point, adding each other to social media. There was some memory of a girl talking to Rob, and her deciding to get another juice before talking to one his biggest streaming rivals. The odd thing about these memories is that it really didn't seem like she was the one performing these actions.

She splashed a little cold water on her face, carefully patting it in away from her eye makeup. She looked in both directions, saw nobody, and adjusted her bra.

Just as she finished, a toilet flushed and out of the stall tumbled Cassie.

Their eyes met and neither moved for a moment. Cassie slowly drew herself upright and strolled over to the sink next to Samantha.

She washed her hands while Samantha finger combed her hair and adjusted her own braids. Cassie dried her hands and started to adjust her dress, lifting and pushing her breasts into place, tugging the hemline up, and pulling the straps to the side.

Samantha cleared her throat. "I like your dress," she said.

Cassie eyed her up and down. "You couldn't pull it off," she finally replied.

She turned, eyes flashing, and stared Cassie down.

"What is your problem?" Samantha demanded.

"Me?!" Cassie responded. "My problem? What is yours? That's the only nice thing you've said to me since we've met, and it was forced."

"Why are you always all over my fiance?" Samantha asked.

Cassie cringed. "I am not! We are friends! We behave like friends! You wouldn't ask Cameron why he's all over Rob."

"That's different," Samantha cried.

"Why?" Cassie asked. "Because I have tits?"

"Oh, those? You have those? Who would've known?! You keep them such a secret, so tucked away!"

"If that's all you notice of me, that is your problem."

"That's all anyone notices! Newsflash: people aren't watching you for the riveting gameplay!" Samantha screamed.

Cassie's face fell. Her lip trembled. Samantha saw weakness and pounced.

"That whole presentation on gender in gaming. Why do men not take women seriously? Why don't more women play games? You! The answer is you! Men idealize female gamers to be bubbly dumb bimbos with their tits out, and other women think they can't be gamers because they aren't whores!"

Cassie turned red. "That's not true!"

"Look at your social media," Samantha continued. "How much of it is gameplay and how much of it is bikini pictures?"

Cassie looked down. Samantha went in for the killing blow.

"How do you think little girls feel when they watch your stream? Do you think they feel empowered? Like they can play games just as good as boys just the way they are? Or do you think they're reaching for their mom's makeup and stuffing tissues down their training bras?"

Cassie stared at Samantha. The voices were swarming, overlapping each other in an excited cacophony. Then, as one whole being, for the first time in a long time, Samantha spoke.

"It's all your fault."

She then stormed out of the bathroom.

As she rounded the corner, her head began to pound. She stumbled back out onto the patio. She felt like throwing up but hoped the air would help. She hadn't meant to spill all of that out on her. She was just trying to be nice with the dress compliment. Now that it was out in the open, now what?

"Rob's going to be livid," a voice whispered. "That's what."

Shit. Rob. Samantha pulled herself together and walked back inside. Sure enough, Cassie was talking to Rob. Her arms were gesticulating wildly, growing more and more frantic. Rob grabbed them and pulled her into a hug as she began to cry.

Samantha felt her own tears well up. She felt betrayed, but worse, she felt guilty. Like she had done something horribly wrong.

She ran outside and pulled up a ride share on her phone.

Once it arrived, she climbed into the backseat and sobbed quietly. If the driver noticed, he didn't say anything. He did stay outside until she had closed the door to the townhouse.

The voices whispered among themselves, but Samantha was silent as she went upstairs. She quietly removed her makeup and showered. She looked at the bed but decided she would be the one on the couch that night. She brushed her teeth, put on some loose shorts and a tshirt and crept back downstairs. She pulled both sofa pillows to the end of the couch and pulled the blanket over her. She turned on cartoons and stared blankly at the screen, not really absorbing what was going on in the animation. At one point, Rob walked in. He didn't say anything but went straight upstairs. Samantha turned her face into the pillows and began to cry.

She wept until her body gave up and pulled her into a deep sleep.

Chapter Twenty-One

The bell rang. My head shot up from its place on the desk.

I was in the classroom again. The walls were bare, except for an impossibly long chalkboard. The desks were spaced far apart in a chessboard pattern and a broken av cart slumped in the corner, the monitor's screen shattered and staring blankly at me. Overhead, the singular hanging dome light cast a pallid yellow sheen onto everything.
Ms. Shirley, in a long polka dot dress, took her place in front of the board.

"Your life essays are due today, class. Please pass them to the front."

Backpacks rustled as my classmates pulled large binders and portfolios out. They wordlessly began to pass them forward, each one thicker and more professional looking than the last. I looked under my desk expecting to find a backpack, but only seeing my own beat up sneakers.

I felt my stomach sink as I sat back up. I raised my hand, and Ms. Shirley sneered at me.

"What is it this time, Samantha?"

I swallowed the lump in my throat.

"I think I left my essay in my locker, ma'am."

The classroom became deafeningly quiet in an instant. The light above my head buzzed and increased in intensity. The ceiling retreated back, and the walls pulled in. The class began to fade at the edges, like a zoom lens had been reconfigured to focus on me.

"Did you now?" the teacher asked. "Or did you not do it?"

My hands began to tremble. I clasped them together and shoved them into my lap.

"I did it. I know I did."

"Don't lie to me, Samantha!"

I winced. The classroom erupted into a gale of giggles and shrieks.

"I'm not lying," I said, tears beginning to stream down my face. "I swear I'm not."

"How can you be so irresponsible?"

I shook my head.

"Why can't you act your age?"

Ms. Shirley was now in front of me. Her hands slammed on top of my desk. I flinched, and the class roared in laughter.

"Why are you such a disappointment?"

"I tried my best, I promise."

"It's not good enough," she hissed.

Her arm shot out, and she slapped me across the face, knocking me to the floor.

"How could you?!" she howled, her voice deepening.

I covered my face with my arms and sobbed. Blows began to rain down on me, and I could feel fingers trying to pry my arms away. Shrill screams, pleading in tone, mixed with low grunts and growls. The laughter rang out from all around.

"Look at what you've done," the deeper voice called out. "Look at what you've done!"

More blows came, seemingly from multiple sources. I yelped as one landed on the base of my spine.

"Oh, it doesn't hurt that much. Grow up!"

The giggling and shrieking rose in volume, but I couldn't see my classmates anymore. I knew if I moved my arms, I was in real danger.

As if picking up on that thought, a large hand entangled itself in my hair and yanked, attempting to wrench my head out into the open. I screamed and lashed out, feeling my fingernails catch flesh. The laughing stopped, as did all the hitting.

I warily opened an eye and peered out from over my arms. I was outside now, surrounded by trees. My classmates and teacher stood, with heads tilted down, assembled like an army around me. Among them, in the center, stood a large, dark figure with three bright red scratches running down where its face would be. Its eyes swirled red and black. I shakily stood up and stared at it, wincing from the pain all the wallops had caused. It regarded me with an air of hostility. Slowly, it tilted its head to the side.

"Run," a voice growled.

I didn't need to be told twice, I turned on my heel and flung myself into the welcoming woods before me. As soon as I did, the laughter and shrieking resumed, and I could hear leaves crunching behind me. I wasn't sure where I was going. After only a minute, my legs and lungs were burning, but I pushed on.

I skittered down hills and hopped over logs. At one point, I stumbled and fell onto all fours. This did not slow me down, as I began to run and leap like an animal, alternately scurrying across the forest floor and jumping high up into the branches. I didn't look behind me, but I could sense danger close by.

In the distance, a fence emerged. I leapt onto a branch and peered down at it. It was an unassuming wire fence with a ditch running alongside it. Beyond that stretched a field with a few broken down cars sinking into the grass.

With a cackle, somebody landed on the branch beside me. I instinctively swung my leg out and kicked them off before springing down myself. I clawed my way up the ditch and clambered over the fence. I took off running into the field towards an older sedan.

I pulled at the door handle, relieved when the door popped and swung open. I shoved myself into the front seat and slammed the door shut. I sank down low, hiding behind the dashboard. I squeezed my eyes shut and wrapped my arms over my head.

I heard a loud rushing sound and felt the car rock. A crack of thunder rang out and raindrops began to beat on the metal roof. I was about to open my eyes when a loud, angry howl filled the air. I yelped and squeezed my eyes shut even tighter.

The howling lasted a few minutes, darting back and forth as if the source were running to and fro. Eventually, it ended, and all that could be heard was the rain. I gave it a moment, just to be safe. I unfolded my arms and sat up, letting my hands fall to the seat under me.

The rain was coming down like a monsoon. Sharp bursts of lightning spiderwebbed across the sky as thunder gently rumbled in the background. I looked down at the dash to find the car was on. I quietly reached out and turned on the radio.

As the smooth sounds of an oldies station took over, I spotted a hint of manila out of the corner of my eye. There, on the driver's seat, was a file folder. I stretched my hand out to touch it, then pulled back as if burned. My eyes darted around wildly, making sure I was alone.

I gingerly picked it up, feeling the weight of it in my hands. I opened it to find a page with a series of dots smeared across it. As I stared, I was pulled in, the world swirling around me and rearranging itself.

I stood inside a small bedroom. On one side, was a crib with a sleeping toddler. On the other was a wooden bed where a small blonde girl was curled up. The small window between the two flashed briefly with lightning.

I was about to step out of the room when the first shout rang out.

An argument began to escalate just outside the room. The girl's eyes fluttered open. She listened to the voices, sometimes hushed, sometimes ringing out. I stared at her, watching her face twist into discomfort. Her lip trembled, and she looked devastated and tired. She pulled a pillow up over head and pressed it down, squishing it down onto her ear in an attempt to drown out the sounds.

Then, a small cry came from the crib. I turned to see the toddler had rolled over and was mumbling something in his sleep. As I waited with bated breath for him to wake up, I heard the bed behind me shift. I turned once more and found myself staring at an entirely different girl.

She was the same stature, same blonde hair, same pink nightgown, but her jaw was set and her eyes flashed with a different sort of personality.

She stood up and pushed past me, checking on the child in the crib. As the argument grew louder, she took a deep breath, clenched her fists, and stepped out into the hallway.

I chased after her, only to get yanked backwards into the car once more. I groped around even before I was fully there, searching for the file folder in vain.

My eyes darted up to the windshield where I saw an umbrella fading into the distance. I reached over from the passenger seat and grabbed the steering wheel. The car lurched forward and began to roll steadily towards the umbrella. I wasn't able to control the speed, but I could aim it.

"I almost had it," I muttered. "I almost had it."

I wasn't sure what it was, but I was close. There was something about that scene that felt like puzzle pieces fitting together. Some element had made sense in the broad scheme of things. If I had stayed longer, would I have fully realized it? The car sped up, but the umbrella continued to fade.

The rain grew heavier, and I could see the trees around the field whipping around wildly. The car suddenly pulled to the left and revved hard. I was flung backwards and scrambled to gain control of the wheel again. Try as I might to turn it to the right, it refused. I watched helplessly as the vehicle ran over hills and through fields, plowing onward with no concern of obstacles. I did see a road coming up and tried tugging on the wheel again.

It turned a little, but not enough to change course entirely. It rolled onto the gravel, and I pushed on the side of the steering wheel, hoping it would want to follow the road.

It did not.

Gravel quickly became dirt again, and the car swerved from left to right and back to center. I let go of the wheel and tried the door, only to find no handle. I looked up through the windshield and began to panic. There was an obviously steep drop off up ahead, and the car was barrelling towards it. I turned back to the door to lower the window, but I couldn't find that either.

As the hood cleared the lip of the drop off and dipped down into thin air, I screamed. There was water below, and it was rushing up towards me so quickly. Right before impact, I closed my eyes. The little girl's face, my face, appeared, changing rapidly into that determined presence.

Chapter Twenty-Two

Samantha woke up to an aching back and numb legs. The couch had not treated her well after all. As she sat up, her spine cracked and her toes popped. She swiveled her head from side to side and extended her arms out as far as they could reach. The sun was peering into the windows, casting long shadows over everything. Samantha could hear Rob's snores tumbling down from upstairs.

She rested her elbows on her knees and sank her head into her hands. It was the last day of the convention. This would be her only chance to make things right.

"Make what right?" a voice asked. "You did nothing wrong!"

"You embarrassed Rob," another argued. "He probably wants nothing to do with you!"

Samantha shook her head and let out a small groan. She knew what she did was wrong; she didn't need anyone else to tell her that.

"But why?" she whispered. Why had she said all of those mean things to Cassie? Did she really mean it?

"Of course you did!" the voice rang out.

Did she? Samantha thought of all the times she had stood up for women when they were accused of being sluts or dressing provocatively. She considered how often she herself had dealt with some sort of sexism surrounding gaming. She felt a deep, stabbing sense of shame. She was just as bad as all of the people she had argued with in the past.

She turned her thoughts to Cassie and felt anger well up inside of her. She had ruined everything. If she didn't exist, the convention would have been fun, and she would have been snuggled up with Rob this morning. Instead, this girl would see her whole life in ruins.

"Does she really care, though?" a voice asked. "Honestly, do you think she even thinks about you?"

Samantha's eyes grew wide. Was she giving Cassie more attention than she was receiving? If Cassie was thinking about Samantha, would she be that flirty with Rob?

"Is she even being flirty?" the voice continued. "Or is it just her online schtick?"

Again, Samantha was taken aback. Her mind swirled, darting between thoughts of angry, misogynistic people and Cassie laughing and posing for pictures. Before the two thought patterns could collide, however, another voice spoke up.

"You should get ready for the convention."

Samantha shook her head again and nodded. She stood up and stretched one last time, feeling all the tendons in her body pull tight. She grabbed her phone, turned, and began to creep up the stairs, trying desperately not to make any noise. When she reached the top, her eyes fell on Rob, fast asleep with the blanket pulled up to his chin. His laptop was in the corner of the bed next to his phone. While it was open, the screen was black, the device having shut down some time ago.

She felt the temptation to fire it up and see what he had been working on right before he fell asleep. She knew the password and the code to his phone, too. She bit her lip and continued on into the bathroom, gently closing the door behind her. She brought up her phone and searched for Rob on social media.

There was no mention of last night's disturbance. There were plenty of pictures of him and Brian hanging out. Samantha grimaced. She didn't like Brian much after that night, especially since she had been left with the impression he didn't care for her much either. Still, Rob looked relatively happy and unbothered. She only spotted Cassie in the background of one picture. She scoured the comments to see if anybody mentioned their run in- they had not. She then scrolled back up and hesitantly clicked on Cassie's tag.

Her page came up, with obligatory swimsuit picture. Samantha snorted lightly to herself; of course it was her profile picture. She scrolled through the information section and landed on her feed. The last post was from an hour before, letting everyone know that she would be on one final panel that day, one about fitness in gaming. It was going to be at ten that morning. Samantha took a deep breath and nodded. She would attend and catch Cassie afterwards. Even if she wasn't entirely sure why, she needed to apologize. She sighed and scrolled some more. All the posts were about how much fun she was having at the convention, with pictures of her with other creators. Samantha blinked. She was posing in those pictures the way she had with Rob- leaning on chests, jumping on backs, blowing kisses. Every single image was Cassie in full, signature flirty style.

Samantha suddenly felt uncomfortable, and that same sense of stabbing shame hit her like a wave. She closed out of the app and set her phone on the counter.

"You would never," a shrill voice spoke out. "The audacity. She should be the one ashamed. Imagine what people think."

Samantha shook it off and began to undress. She turned on the shower and let it run while staring at herself in the mirror. Of course she wouldn't; taking one look at herself told her all she needed to know. She was fat and ugly. She would never in a million years get away with the things Cassie did. They were on completely different levels.

"Got a bit of a crush?" a voice teased.

Samantha frowned. "No," she said aloud, throwing herself into the shower.
As she shampooed her hair, her thoughts did turn back to it and to Cassie asking if she would have a problem with a guy hanging out with Rob the way she did. She knew there was an equal chance of him leaving her for either one, so why was it not okay?

"Because she's hot," the same voice teased again.

Samantha hung her head as her face reddened. It really was that simple. She was jealous. As she scrubbed, she began to think of the other areas Cassie had her beat in: gaming, socializing, humor, fitness. She was everything Samantha had pretended to be when writing that list in her notebook, and if that list was supposed to make Samantha the perfect match for Rob, then Cassie really was just that.

She stepped out of the shower and started to towel off. She really did owe Cassie an apology. She blushed again, thinking back on her outbursts. She was ashamed of what had happened and wondered if Cassie would even speak to her long enough for an apology to be made. She wrapped the towel around herself and opened the door.

Rob was sitting up in bed, typing away at his laptop. He looked up long enough to make eye contact, then moved his gaze back down. Samantha swallowed the lump in her throat and opened her bag, pulling out a knotted tee and some leggings.

"Rob," she said, voice breaking, eyes still trained on her bag as she fished around for socks and underwear.

He didn't answer, but he did stop typing.

"Rob, I'm sorry," she continued. "I am so ashamed and embarrassed by what I've done. I'm going to talk to Cassie and make things right. I'm so sorry for what I've done to you."

He was silent, so she slowly lifted her eyes. He was staring straight ahead with a distant look.

Samantha nodded and stood up with her clothes. "If you don't want to talk, I understand. I wouldn't want to talk to me, either. I'll start packing when we get home, just let me know what you want to keep from the trip."

She turned towards the bathroom.

"Why?" Rob asked quietly.

She stopped and slowly turned. He was looking at her now, still somber, but at least looking at her.

"Why what?" she asked.
"Packing? For what?" he continued.

She shrugged. "I didn't think you'd want me around."

Rob sighed and pinched the bridge of his nose.

"I mean, with how awful I've been," she said nervously, "especially towards Cassie, and I see now that she really is an amazing person, and I'm terrible, and I-"

"Stop," Rob commanded. Samantha fell silent.

"Do you really think I want you to go away?" he asked.

Samantha nodded, tears beginning to well up in her eyes.

He sighed again. "I don't want you to leave," he said. "I just worry about you."

Samantha shook her head. "Why?"

"You're so smart," he replied. "You're funny, and you're beautiful. You're my other half. I hate that you can't see that. I hate that you think you're inferior to anyone. Am I embarrassed by your outburst the other night? Yes, but everyone has been flooding my messages asking about you, making sure you're alright. Cassie and I are the only ones who know about last night, and I convinced her that you were under a lot of stress. She's even asked how you're doing. As far as anyone is concerned, you're nervous about starting your channel and have been dealing with a bunch of stress at work."

"Thank you," she mumbled. "I'm-"

"Don't say it," he interrupted. "Just promise me you'll get some help when we get home."

Samantha nodded, tears slipping down her face. She turned back to the bathroom and placed her hand on the knob.

"I love you," Rob said behind her.

She smiled a little. "I love you, too," she replied.

As she got dressed and did her hair and makeup, the voices swelled in her head. They argued as to whether he really meant what he said, if they were going to be okay, and if she really needed to seek help.

"Again, if I can hear you, I need help," she thought.

"That's what you think," a voice challenged her.

She shook her head and continued getting ready. Rob walked in at one point and started brushing his teeth.

"Did you want breakfast?" she asked.

Rob shook his head and spit out the toothpaste. "Got a few meetings this morning. I'm actually running a bit behind."

"Okay," she said. "Meet up for lunch?"

He nodded and put a hand on her shoulder.

"I'm serious," he said. "I love you, and I'm worried about you."

Samantha sighed and nodded. "I know. I'll talk to Cassie while we're here, and then I'll get help."

"A therapist?" he asked.

"Yes," she replied. "I promise."

Rob kissed her temple and tugged her hair before returning to the bedroom to find clothes for the day. Samantha put the finishing touches on and grabbed her bag.

"I'll order a ride," Rob said as he tugged on a pair of pants, "if you want to meet me downstairs."

Samantha nodded and moved towards the stairs. Right in front of her was Rob's open laptop. She could see the messages displayed on it, a back and forth between him and Cassie. As much as she wanted to see what was being written, she fixed her eyes ahead of her and continued on her way.

By the time Rob made it downstairs, the car had pulled up. They got in and thanked the driver. When he replied, Samantha's gaze flew up to the driver's seat. It was the man from the night before.

His eyes met hers in the rearview mirror, and he gave her a little nod. She awkwardly nodded back.

The entire way there, Rob attempted small talk, but the man driving would not engage. Instead, he glanced furtively at Samantha, a confused and concerned look on his face. Samantha would smile and nod back, trying to show that she was okay and dispel any thoughts that Rob may have been involved in last night's fiasco. When they pulled up to the convention center, though, he still had the same look on his face.

They waved goodbye and made their way inside. Rob immediately began to jog into the showroom, checking his phone as he did. Samantha shuffled up to a large map and searched for the room she needed to go to for the panel.

"Need help?" a voice asked from behind her.

She turned to find Cassie standing there, also in a knotted shirt and leggings.

"Nice outfit," she said quietly, putting on an awkward smile.

Cassie glared at her.

Samantha sighed. Before she could say anything, though, Cassie rolled her eyes.

"Look, I get that you're under a lot of pressure or whatever, but that doesn't excuse what you've said to and about me."

Samantha nodded. "I know," she whispered.

Cassie raised an eyebrow. Samantha drew in a deep breath and met her gaze.

"I'm sorry," she said firmly.

Cassie shook her head. "I'm too hungover for this shit."

She turned to leave, but Samantha grabbed her arm. She looked back at her.

"Really," Samantha said. "I've thought about it, and I'm sorry. I had no right to say any of those things to you."

Cassie yanked her arm away. "Then why did you?"

Samantha's mouth gaped open. The voices swirled again, each of them suggesting a different answer. The room began to blur around the edges, but Samantha closed her mouth and bit down on her lip, bringing everything back into focus.

"I was afraid," she admitted.

Cassie's head tilted. "Afraid? Of me? What do you mean?"

Samantha blinked and considered how to proceed.

Cassie stared at her, then started to laugh.

"Oh no," she said. "Oh my god, you thought that I was going to take Rob away from you, didn't you?"

Samantha looked down and blushed. Cassie began to cackle, letting out a snort every once in a while.

"Holy shit. No. No offence to Rob, but have you seen the men I date?"

Samantha's head shot up with an offended look spread across her face.

"Me and Rob? He's like my brother. He's not my type at all. Oh my goodness, you're killing me. I am way too hungover for this."

She spun around and waved a hand in the air.

"Insecure bitches, I swear" she called out.

Samantha stood rooted to the spot. She wasn't sure how to process any of what just happened. Did that conversation really count as an apology? Should it have? She suddenly felt like launching into her again but told herself to let go.

"There are better ways about this," a voice reassured her calmly.

"Beat her at her own game!" another hyped her up. "You can get her numbers easy!"

"Or call her out at her panel," yet another seethed. "Tell everyone about the whore little miss snark really is."

"Okay, that's enough," a final voice replied. "Let's stay far away from that panel."

Samantha nodded. She could agree with that, at least. She turned back to the map, looking at the listing of rooms. Her eyes were slowly drawn to a small pink room outlined in blue in the upper corner of the map. She smiled, readjusted her bag, and turned towards the escalators. She trekked past a variety of people, families with excited children, people in costume taking pictures, others in branded polos exchanging cards. She turned the corner and took a deep, relaxing breath before stepping inside.

The quiet room was exactly as she remembered, albeit with fewer people than there was before. She saw the lady from earlier and nodded at her. She got a smile and a wave back. There were a few beanbags empty, so Samantha walked over to one and settled down in it. She set her phone to vibrate and her alarm for noon, as she and Rob had decided to meet then for lunch.

She pulled up a webcomic on her phone and began to scroll through it. As the colorful pictures scrolled past, her eyes began to slide shut.

Chapter Twenty-Three

My eyes opened to a white canopy. I resisted sitting up, only because the bed I was in was so comfortable. I yawned and rolled over, rubbing my fists into my eyes. With a loud, contented sigh, and one final stretch, I opened my eyes once more.

"Good morning, sunshine," Eric said, smiling at me.

I jumped and almost fell out of bed.

He laughed from his perch on the edge.

"It's not nice to startle someone like that," Ariana said languidly. I looked up to see her standing at the windowsill, looking out over the sea. I was back in the blue room.

"Ah, it was just a little joke," he reassured her, "and she's fine. Bed's too big to fall out of, am I right, Sam?"

I sat up and shook my head to clear out the cobwebs. "Looks that way," I agreed.

I pulled the blankets up around my waist and smoothed the sleeves of the white nightgown I wore. "Why are we here?" I asked.

"It's what you needed," Eric answered.

"You had a rough night and tough morning," Ariana added. "Now it's time to relax."

"What about the panic eyes?" I asked.

Eric shook his head. "Not here," he said. "This is a safe place."

I nodded slowly, letting it sink in.

"We're all proud of you," Ariana said. "Even though some of us may not admit it."

"What for?" I asked.

She turned to look at me, coppery eyes flashing in the sunlight pouring in. "You discovered a lot about yourself," she said. "You were brave enough to take control of the situation."
Eric leaned forward, "Of course, we still hate her."

Ariana waved the thought off. "Of course. Completely uncalled for on her part, all of it, but you were willing to admit that you were afraid. That takes a lot."

I smiled at her. "Thank you," I said.

She stared at me. "Next time, let me handle it," she said, and turned back to the window.

Before I could ask what she meant, Eric leaned over and grabbed my hand.

"Speaking of handling it, did you get our gift?"

"Your gift?" I repeated.

"A certain," he winked, "file folder."

"Oh!" I cried. "That was you?"

"Shhhh!" he said, lifting a finger to his grin. "Not so loud."

"His idea, my doing," Ariana clarified.

"Yes, yes I did," I said.

"Did it help?" he asked.

I pondered it for a moment. I had made the connection, but would that help me with the little girl? I wasn't sure I was ready for another run in with the panic eyed monster.

"We couldn't get you all of them," Eric continued, looking defeated, "but we thought one might help."

I put my other hand over his. "It did help," I insisted. "Thank you for doing that."

He smiled and looked over at Ariana. "See, it was worth it," he said.

I smiled back at him but felt my heart sank. What did they have to go through to get that file?

Eric looked at me with concern.

"Don't worry about it," he said. "Just relax."

I nodded and settled myself into the bed, pulling a pillow up behind my back.

Eric and Ariana began to chat back and forth about the convention, picking at one another, as I stared out the window. A storm was blowing in over the sea. I knew an omen when I saw one.

Chapter Twenty-Four

The buzzing in her hand woke Samantha. She opened a bleary eye and turned her phone's alarm off. She hadn't realized how tired she was until she had nodded off over the webcomic.

She stood up, her knees popping loudly. She looked around at the concerned gazes sheepishly, and ducked out of the room.

They had decided to meet by the front entrance, and Samantha could already see Rob from the escalator. His gaze was buried in his phone, his thumb swiping the screen periodically. Samantha smoothed her shirt over her stomach and nervously tugged at her ponytail. The interaction with Cassie began to play back in her mind, and her brow furrowed. She turned a more critical gaze towards Rob.

He was tall, messy brown hair already streaked with grey and had a rough, shadowy beard. He had a bit of a stomach, but it made him look more comforting, more like a bear ready to cuddle than anything. His face was naturally set into a brooding scowl, but when he was excited about something, which was more often than not, it lit up, and his green eyes would sparkle and dance like electricity. He was a big, loud guy, and as Cassie had pointed out, not at all like the compact, quiet men that she was often seen with.

Samantha pondered this further. Cassie was very much into image. Rob had often talked about her hustle when it came to marketing and self promotion. Every post, every bikini photo, every wardrobe malfunction was carefully calculated to bring in more people to her audience. Likewise, the men that she chose to associate with romantically had to be carefully considered, as well. They had to be an audience attractor, as well, without being too threatening to the perceived connection her fans had with her. Samantha had no doubt that Cassie also found these men attractive, that they were her "type". When comparing her relationship with Rob, there was more in common than not. Rob was boisterous, a people person, and shone in the spotlight. Cassie was very much the same, basking in attention and thriving in social settings. Samantha, on the other hand, was often quiet and withdrawn; social settings made her nervous, unless she already knew the people involved. Perhaps this made her, and by default, those smaller, quieter men, the proverbial other half to these social creatures.

Samantha smiled a little. She felt like she had cracked the case. She should not be worried about Cassie. Rob was not her type, Samantha was definitely Rob's type, and she trusted him completely.

She stepped off the escalator and made her way over to him. As she drew closer, she saw that he was scrolling through pictures of a girl. She blinked but steadied herself in her recently acquired knowledge. Once she was close enough, she could see the girl more clearly. She was very curvy, with wide hips and a full chest. She had long brown hair and wore tiny shorts and skirts with the type of nerdy shirts being sold at booths in the next room. Samantha cleared her throat and smiled up at Rob.

He looked over at her, startled, and ran a hand through his hair.

"Hey, Sam. Ready for lunch?"

Samantha nodded. "Absolutely! Did you meet someone new?" she asked, motioning towards his phone.

Rob furrowed his brow in confusion, then looked at the screen.

"Oh!" he exclaimed. "That's Emily Chaos."

He looked at her as if she should know who that was. Samantha turned her head and raised her eyebrow. Rob's face fell into confusion, then realization.

"We kept bumping into each other at the different panels and meetings," he explained. "We were also at the same booths at the time a lot, so we swapped cards. Turns out, she's a sci-fi gamer, too! We're planning on co-streaming later this week, since that terraforming game I told you about is going to be releasing a new patch."

Samantha had no idea what game he was talking about but nodded.

"She sounds cool," she said slowly.

"She is!" Rob continued. "You would like her a lot. You have a lot in common. She's kinda quiet and shy, but she's very smart and funny. She also likes darker stuff, you know? She does horror games when she's not doing sci-fi."

Samantha swallowed the lump that had formed in her throat. A very familiar bubbling rose up in her stomach, and voices started to become clear in her head.

"She's the opposite of Cassie," one whispered. "Isn't that what Rob is into?"

"Did you see those pictures?" another added. "She's gorgeous!"

"Rob is definitely going to leave us," yet another claimed. "She's everything we are and more!"

Samantha gave Rob a nervous laugh. "Yeah, we'll have to hang out sometime."

Rob's eyebrows jumped. "Oh! We could invite her out to lunch! Let me text her and see what she's doing."

He pulled up his messages, and Samantha saw that they had already been exchanging dozens of texts. She put a hand on his arm and shook her head.

"It's cool," she said lightly. "She's probably busy wrapping up stuff, and besides, the signal in here sucks anyway. We can catch her later. I'm super hungry right now."

Rob turned his phone off and slid it into his pocket.

"Yeah, you're right," he said. "Besides, she only lives about an hour away! Maybe you two could take a girl's trip at some point."

Samantha felt the blood drain from her face.

"Maybe," she said, pulling an awkward smile.

"She's close enough to drive to," a voice perked up.

"It makes her more real," another added.

"Oh, for sure," the first replied. "What are we going to do?"

"Nothing. We are going to do nothing," a stern voice interjected. "Leave it."

Samantha closed her eyes and took a deep breath. When she opened them, Rob was looking at her with concern.

"Are you okay?" he asked.

Samantha nodded. "Yep, just tired. My people batteries are low."

Rob nodded back. "Got it. You weird introvert you!"

He slung an arm around her shoulder and kissed the top of her head.

"Let's get some food," he said, guiding her out of the convention center.

They wandered down the sidewalk, passing groups of people with lanyards and backpacks. Everyone looked drained but happy. It must have been a long week for many of them, as well, Samantha reckoned.

They spotted a sports bar that seemed to be clearing out and ducked in. After a few minutes of waiting, they were guided to a tiny table equipped with rickety bar stools.

Rob shifted in his seat. "The food must be really good," he said, opening up a menu.

Samantha picked a splinter off the edge of the table. "Must be," she agreed.

The menu was short on food, offering up the typical bar fare of fried carbs and battered vegetables. The beer list, however, was impressively long and boasted brews from around the world.

Rob's eyes lit up, and he looked at Samantha nervously.

"Would you mind?" he asked, gesturing to the list.

She shook her head. "Go for it! I'm going to stick to soda, I think."

Rob grinned and eagerly returned to the menu.

Samantha felt her stomach sink a little. In truth, she would have liked to grab a stout or a hefeweizen, but she understood that her actions over the past few days prevented her from doing so, especially with Rob present.

"Baby steps," a voice calmly reassured her. "Baby steps to being a better person."

Samantha nodded and looked back down at the menu.

As it turned out, the food was delicious. Samantha had started off staring longingly at Rob's beer, but soon found herself preoccupied with mozzarella sticks and cheddar peppers. She barely noticed when Rob jumped up and ran over to the door.

"Hey, Sam!" a familiar voice called out.

She turned, cheese strung down from her mouth and across her chin. Jason and Todd waved at her as they approached the table, led by Rob. She hastily cleaned herself up and looked around anxiously for extra stools.

Jason knew exactly what she was doing and shook his head. "We're good; we just wanted to stop by before we left."
Samantha tilted her head. "How did you know where we were?"

Todd tapped his temple. "Telepathy."

Jason and Rob screamed with laughter. Samantha nodded her head slowly, confused.

Rob wiped his eyes and waved a hand in the air. "You missed it! At lunch the other day, Brian, oh lord, Brian, he-"

Jason grabbed his shoulder. "He, this girl, she-"

They collapsed into laughter again.

Samantha pulled her lips tight and looked down at her plate. How many little things had she missed over the past few days?

Todd shook his head. "Anyway, we saw Rob's post, and we didn't want to leave without saying goodbye.

Jason wrapped his arm around Rob. "It was great seeing you guys, and we can't wait for the next one!"

Todd reached out to Samantha, and she gingerly gave him a hug. She no longer knew quite where she stood with everyone.

Jason pulled them both into a giant group hug with his other arm.

"Ugh, I hate when these things end," he said.

"There is one final meet up at the convention in about an hour," Rob offered.

Jason waved a hand at him. "No, sorry, man. We've got to get on the road."

Todd nodded. "Work always starts bright and early after a convention."

Jason whispered conspiratorially in Samantha's ear, "with a little help of some special coffee, if you catch my drift."

She laughed and hugged him back.

They did wait for Samantha and Rob to finish their lunch and left the bar together. Their conversation was light and easy flowing, and it made Samantha feel much more comfortable with how the past week had gone. Perhaps she hadn't completely ruined everything.

They said their goodbyes, and Rob and Samantha headed back into the convention center. Rob checked the time.

"We've got a few minutes. Did you want to do anything before we meet up with people?"

Samantha thought about it. "No," she said. "The booths are probably cleared out."

Rob nodded. "I checked this morning and they were all wrapping up."

Samantha shrugged. "We can just go wait. Where is the meet up?"

Rob raised an eyebrow and pointed towards the lobby. "It's by the entry display. You said you were going to climb it and be the person in the logo for the picture."

Samantha's eyes widened. "I never said that!"

Rob nodded again. "Yes, you did," he insisted. "The first day we were here. You and Paige talked about it. She thought it would be a cute way to start off your streaming."

Samantha's heart began to race. She bit her lip and nodded. "Oh, that conversation! Right!"

"It's been a crazy week," Rob reassured her.

"It sure has," she agreed.

They slowly waded through the crowd of people leaving. A few members of Rob's circle were already waiting there and eagerly greeted them as they walked up. Rob broke off from Samantha and began to take a few selfies and smaller group pictures with the men who were there. Samantha sighed and opened up her phone. There was barely any signal, but she figured she could wait for things to load.

As she watched the spinning circle on her screen, she heard a familiar screech.

"Oh my god, ROB!"

She looked up to see Cassie running over. Her breath caught in her chest, and her head began to feel fuzzy.

Rob opened his arms. "Cassie!"

She slowed her run and strolled over to him.

"How's it going, big guy?" she asked and gave him a high five.

"Great!" he said. "You joining in for the picture?"

"Wouldn't miss it!" she exclaimed.

She turned her head and met Samantha's gaze.

"Hey, girl!" she said, smiling wide.

Samantha's whole body erupted into a chill.

"Hi," she replied weakly.

"How was the rest of your day? I saw you went to that bar! Was it good?"

Samantha's head began to fill with static. She felt a shift, like she was being thrown into a passenger seat.

She felt her lips curve into a smile.

"Girl, you wouldn't believe the food they had!" she found herself saying with a flirty tone.

Cassie's eyes lit up. "Yeah? Tell me about it."

"Cheese," Samantha replied with a raised eyebrow. "Cheese for days."

Cassie laughed and walked over. "That sounds like heaven! Do you know, I refuse to eat cheese most days?"

Samantha shook her head. "What? Why?"

Cassie patted her stomach. "So many reasons, girl. One is that I can't stop when I start."

They giggled, and Cassie snaked an arm around Samantha's shoulders. Inside, she recoiled and felt panicky. On the outside, her body leaned into the contact, and she wrapped an arm around Cassie's waist.

"Ooh, let's get a selfie!" Cassie exclaimed.

"Yes!" Samantha replied excitedly. "Just us girls!"

They took a whole series of pictures together, a few fun, a few serious, and a few flirty.

Cassie skimmed through her phone. "These are perfect. Just what I need for my feed."

She looked up at Samantha. "And just what you needed to for your side of things."

Samantha felt the shift again but found herself still forced to watch her own actions.

"And what does that mean?" she asked in a measured voice, squaring her shoulders.

Cassie smirked. "You know exactly what it means. You're welcome."

With that, she turned and cried out another person's name and ran off to see them.

Samantha felt the fuzzy feeling start to fade and began to settle back into her body.

Paige and Josh walked up with Sarah and Cameron.

"We missed you at the burger joint!" Sarah said.

"We thought you were going there," Josh agreed. "Why did you go to that shady bar?"

Cameron crossed his arms. "Was Rob not feeling it?"

Samantha shrugged. "I don't know," she said. "It just seemed like an interesting place."

Paige smiled. "No worries," she replied. "Just let us know next time you change plans."

Samantha blinked, confused, but let it roll off of her. Eventually, the lobby filled up with people wanting to join the photo. As promised, Samantha climbed her way up the back and leaned out with a big grin on her face. They snapped a few photos like that before security showed up and asked her to get down. She then found herself shuffled between Rob and Brian, and they took several more pictures.

When the camera lowered, a collective sigh escaped the crowd. Now it was time to pack up and return to their day-to-day lives.

There were many hugs and a few tears, and Samantha stood awkwardly to the side, watching it all.

She and Rob eventually made it back to their townhome and loaded everything into the car. She collected the garbage bags from that infamous night and, with embarrassment and shame, added them to the large trash bin outside.

She slid into the passenger seat and watched Rob put the key away before getting into the driver's seat. He started the car, and Samantha felt a sudden release in her body. All the tension in her legs and shoulders escaped, and she settled back into the chair.

Rob put a hand on her thigh. "You okay?" he asked.

"Yeah," she replied. "Just tired."

She leaned her head against the window and watched the landscape go by, her eyes slowly sliding shut.

Chapter Twenty-Five

I felt water drip on my head and waved it away. Another drop hit my arm, then another on my neck. I slowly opened my eyes and took in my surroundings.

I was on the main street, curled up on a bench. The air was cool, and the wind whipped wildly. Overhead, dark clouds swirled menacingly. The rain hadn't quite started, but a few droplets were being released and hitting the ground. The flowers were in full bloom, almost defiantly so, and nodded with the beat of the wind.

A low, mournful tune filled the street. I looked over at one of the shop windows and saw the cat playing his piano, his head tilted in a curious manner. Next to the door sat a shiny blue bicycle, it's seat and tires restored to a healthy brilliance.
I looked down the other side of the street and saw Eric and Ariana. They looked nervous. I stood up and walked over to them.

"Hey, guys, what's up?" I asked.

Eric smiled apprehensively.

"How are you feeling?" he asked.

"I'm feeling great," I replied.

"Are you sure?" Ariana asked.

I frowned. "Why do you ask?"

She pointed at the sky. "The storm's coming."

"The storm is here," a voice chimed in from behind me.

I turned to find Thomas standing there, umbrella closed, but held loosely in his right hand.

"We don't have much time," he continued. "We need to get back to the tower."

I shook my head. "Or what?"

He blinked. "What do you mean "or what"? There was no question. We're almost out of time."

I shrugged. "Before what?"

Thomas opened his mouth and then closed it. He gestured at Eric and Ariana.

"This is on you. You told her too much."

"About what?" I asked.

He ignored me.

"Now the whole system is out of whack. It's going to take extreme measures to fix."

"Fix what?" I demanded.

"Everything," he replied and grabbed my arm.

I wrestled it back and took a step closer to Eric and Ariana.

"I'm not going."

Thomas sighed and raised his left hand to his nose. "You have to. The storm is here."

"What does that even mean?" I asked. "I like storms!"

"Not these kinds," he replied.

"How would you know?" I cried out.

"I just do," he said sadly, and lifted the umbrella.

Out of nowhere, Charity grabbed it and pulled it from his hand.

Thomas scrambled after her, but she held it just out of reach.

"No!" she said. "We need to know what happens."

She tossed the umbrella to Eric.

Thomas lurched towards him, but he danced out of the way.

"You have to trust me," he said, desperately grabbing for the umbrella. "You don't want to be here for what comes next."

Eric shook his head and passed the umbrella to Ariana.

Thomas squared up. He looked at Ariana and sighed.

"You know what needs to be done," he said.

Ariana nodded.

"She needs to be protected," he continued. "She can't go through this."

Ariana took a deep breath. "She can't go through this alone."

Thomas shook his head. "No, Ariana, you know better than this."

"I can protect her," she asserted. "If she wants to know what happens next, then I will make sure she is safe when it happens."

Thomas began to say something, but he stopped, his eyes growing wide. I followed his gaze to a point behind Ariana. There stood a small, white mouse, eagerly cleaning its whiskers.

"Fuck," Thomas said in a hushed tone.

It squeaked, almost as if in response, and took off running down the street past us. We turned and watched it come to a stop. A small hand scooped it up, and the little girl with the panic eyes cuddled it close to her chest.

She looked up at me with a blank expression. I took a step forward.

"Please don't," Thomas said.

I ignored him and took another. The little girl tilted her head, and the mouse swiped at his ears. They both had their eyes trained on me.

I heard the laughing and screeching coming from around the corner. I knew they were on the way. I quickened my pace, but the street began to stretch.

"No!" I screamed, pumping my legs faster.

Behind me, I could hear a clamoring of voices. I strained against whatever was holding me back. The noise behind the little girl became louder, and a shadowy figure began to form behind her. Lightning zig zagged across the sky, and the thunder from it shook the street. Rain began to pelt down, drowning everything. The planters filled with water, and the flowers bent to the soil. The street began to flood, the rushing waves echoing off the buildings. I could no longer hear the piano, but I could hear a faint wailing above the thunder and rain.

Suddenly, something snapped, and the street came reeling back. I stumbled and fell, the water splashing around me and soaking the dress I was wearing.

I turned my head to find Charity and Ariana each holding one of Thomas's arms, while Eric clutched the umbrella to his chest. Tears ran down Thomas's face, and he shook his head.

"Don't do this," he called out. "It's not worth it."

I stood up and turned to face the girl. The crowd had begun to fill in around her. I was scared, but I knew I had to push it aside. I knew who she was.

I moved forward, but so did the shadowy figure, it's eyes swirling maliciously. The crowd careened towards me, but stopped just behind the little girl.

The shadowy figure growled, and I heard its voice echo out above the thunder.

"Run."

I shook my head, my heart pumping in my chest.

"No!" I cried out defiantly and continued to walk forward.

The wailing grew louder, and the little girl's grip on the mouse tightened.

The figure's hands balled into fists.

"RUN!" it commanded. The crowd yelled and screamed incoherently, pushing at whatever barrier they were behind.

I shook my head and shakily moved forward. I was now just a few feet from the little girl.

She looked at me with a terrified expression. She held her hand out to me, shakily.

The shadowy figure stepped towards her and raised its fists.

"You can't stop this! Run!"

"No," I called out, my voice catching in my throat. "I can't stop this, because this has already happened."

It faltered. The little girl blinked at me, her own eyes swirling frantically.

"I can't go back in time and stop you from hurting her," I said, "from giving her the panic eyes. She's already infected."

It laughed and raised its fists again.

"But I can help her!" I yelled. "I can be there for her! I can be who she needed when you gave her those eyes!"

With that, I grabbed her hand and yanked her towards me, pulling her head into my chest. Lightning struck the figure, and it screamed. The crowd fell to ground, clutching their heads and clawing at their eyes. Thunder once again shook the street, causing some of the buildings to crumble and glass to shatter. The rain fell even faster, and I could feel the water splashing at my knees. I picked the little girl up and held her closer, smoothing her blonde hair with one hand and gripping her leg with the other. I closed my eyes and waited for something awful to happen.

Instead, the wailing stopped. The world grew quiet, and I felt the rain fade away. I slowly opened my eyes and found myself in the tower, inside the file room. The wall had been clawed open, and the room outside was dark. The only light came from a single bulb above me, and it illuminated stacks of files flung haphazardly around the space.

I gingerly set the little girl down. She stared up at me quietly, her eyes settling into a quiet, lava lamp like pattern. The mouse squeaked and ran in a circle in her hands.

"I'm sorry," I whispered.

She blinked at me.

"I'm so sorry," I whispered again. "I'm sorry for whatever happened to give you those eyes. I'm sorry I wasn't there for you before. I'm so sorry."

I rested a hand on her head.

"I'm here for you," I said. "Whatever you need, I'm here. I will always take your hand. You don't have to worry about that monster now. You're safe now."

I took a deep breath.

"We're safe now."

The little girl smiled for the first time, her eyes scrunching up on the ends, her cheeks full and pink. She look relieved, like a large weight had been lifted.

"I'm sorry," a voice chimed in.

I turned as Thomas stepped into the light.

"I didn't think you were ready," he said.

I looked at him. "I understand," I said. "I mean, I don't, really, but I know you meant no harm."

He nodded. His head turned to the little girl, and he kneeled before her.

"May I?" he asked, holding his hand out.

She looked at me warily. I nodded, and she slowly handed him the mouse.

"How did she get those eyes?" I asked.

Thomas shook his head. "Some things are best left unsaid."

"But if she's me, and she is, isn't she?" I asked.

He remained silent, stroking the mouse's head.

"I'm sure she is. What happened?" I continued.

He shook his head again.

"And the mouse? Why the mouse?"

Thomas set the mouse on my shoulder and held my hands. "The mouse is a helper," he said quietly. "A very special helper."

The little girl nodded and picked a file up from the floor. She held it out to me.

I took it from her and opened it. It fell open to a page with symbols strewn across it. I felt a familiar tugging and immediately shut it.

"I- I don't want to know," I said decidedly.

Thomas nodded. "And that is why the mouse."

It clambered up my shoulder, standing up to reach into my ear. I felt it begin to burrow, and I instinctively moved to claw at it. Thomas gripped my hands more tightly.

"Let it do its work," he said.

I could feel it clawing and chewing, severing connections. As it did so, I looked back down at the little girl and began to cry.

"I'm sorry," I said.

She hugged me around my knees, and Thomas moved to wrap his arms around me. As the mouse worked its way through my head, my eyes fell closed, and I felt other hands and arms join in, some from high up, some from down below, some small, and some large. They embraced me and shushed me, and I slowly drifted away, faces and names turning to dust in my wake.

Epilogue

Samantha jerked awake to the sound of her alarm blaring. She tiredly rolled over and shut it off, groaning before pulling the blanket back over her head.

"You're going to be late," a voice chided.

"Don't care," she grumbled.

She heard the bedroom door open, and the blankets were ripped off of her. She shrieked and clutched her pillow.

"Rise and shine, sleepyhead!" Rob cried out. "It's the big day!"

"Five more minutes," she whined.

"You had five more minutes an hour ago," Rob said. "I've made you coffee. Get up."

He left, and Samantha slowly sat up. She groaned again but pulled herself out of bed. She sleepily scanned the clothes in her closet, but nothing looked appropriate. She finally settled on some jeans, a tank top, and a long, black sweater.

She shuffled into the bathroom and began her morning routine. As she did so, she tried very hard to remember what she had been dreaming about. She knew it was a nightmare, and there had been a tall, blond guy, but that was all she could recall.

She threw her hair into a bun and did some light makeup. She wanted to look nice, but knew that heavy makeup was probably not a great idea.

She went out into the kitchen and poured a cup of coffee.

"Thank you," she said to Rob as she sat down.

"No worries," he replied, scrolling through his social media. Samantha caught a few of Emily's posts and flinched.

"How's Emily doing?" she asked tentatively.

"Not great," he said. "She wants to have a night out soon, if you're interested in going."

Samantha nodded. "I'll think about it."

Rob looked up at her. "I know you have to go soon, but were you going to eat anything?"

Samantha shook her head. "Nope. Too nervous."

Rob got up and hugged her. "There's nothing to be worried about," he reassured her.

Samantha nodded, but her stomach remained in knots.

"I should go now, anyway," she said, "in case I get lost or turned around."

Rob smiled at her and gave her one more hug. "I love you," he said.

"I love you, too," Samantha replied.

She finished her coffee and set her cup in the sink. The clinking sound made her flinch.

She nervously looked at Rob, but his focus was already back to his phone.

With a sigh, she put on her shoes and headed out to her car. She pulled up the address on her gps and took off.

Her breathing was shallow, and her head began to grow fuzzy. She took a deep breath and turned up the music. Sure enough, she did take a wrong turn. She swore quietly and, with shaking hands, turned the car around.

She pulled into a quiet brick-layed drive lined with trees that gave everything a calm shadowy feel. As she drove, she peered out the windows at the buildings that sprinkled the area. All the people she saw looked content and healthy. They were walking around, looking at squirrels, or talking in clusters as they made their way back to their own cars.

Samantha found herself back at the entrance of the drive. She cursed again and got back on the loop. This time, she spotted the building she needed and pulled into a spot. She shut the engine off and checked the time. It was nearly ten, just in time.

She took a deep breath and looked in the rearview mirror.

"Help me," she thought.

"You've got this," a strong, calm voice replied. "We're with you."

She nodded and stepped out of the car. She climbed the stairs and nearly bumped into a lady coming outside.

"Oh! I'm sorry, sweetheart," the lady said, holding the door for her.

"Um, that's- that's fine," Samantha stammered. "Thank you."

"Last chance to run," a voice whispered.

Samantha swallowed the lump in her throat and stepped inside.

The waiting room was quiet and cozy, not the clinical space she had expected. She daintily perched on the edge of a couch and looked around at the rug and the pictures on the wall. It seemed like a warm, welcoming living room.

"Samantha?" a voice called, this time from outside of her head.

She turned to see another lady in a pale blue shirt standing with a notebook. She had kind eyes that looked a bit concerned.

"Yes," she said. "That's me."

The lady smiled. "Nice to meet you, Samantha, I'm Thea. Please, come with me."

Samantha followed her down a hallway. Thea led her into a room with two large, brown chairs, and a wide window overlooking a cluster of trees and rocks. There was a comfortable looking couch and many books. The space, much like the waiting room, was welcoming and unintimidating.

Samantha took an anxious seat on one of the chairs, and Thea closed the door. She sat down in the other chair and opened her notebook.

"Thank you so much for coming in today," she said. "How are you feeling?"

Samantha swallowed as the voices swirled in her head. She looked at Thea and considered her next words carefully.

"Nervous."

Acknowledgments

This book is incredibly personal to me. It is the first of (hopefully!) many, and likewise, I have many people to thank for its existence.

To my mom and my aunt, thank you for always being my biggest fans. Thank you for powering through those cliffhangers each week and for the feedback. To my dear aunt, I loved reviewing your notes, Aunt Gabbi, and taking time to make those corrections. Mom, I will always cherish your excitement when you realized what the shifting point of view meant. Your encouragement for me to make bold decisions is always appreciated.

To my therapist, my writing cheerleader, thank you for all the support you've given me. From day one in your office, I knew you were the right fit, and although I was scared about the journey ahead of me, you have made the progress both manageable and eye-opening. Thank you for hearing all of me.

To my partner, Paul, thank you for your patience and pleasant nihilism. You've always encouraged me to write and create in whatever medium I was obsessed with at the time. You've seen me at my worst and still chose to love me as I am. We've grown together, come out of the proverbial closet together, and I imagine we will continue to do great things together. Simply put, Paul, I don't hate you.

To my dad and brothers, thank you for being proud of me. Our upbringing wasn't all sunshine and roses, but you've always supported my creative endeavors. You always saw me as a writer. Dad, I will always remember that life isn't perfect, that my efforts are good enough, and to do the work before the play. My little brothers, my playtesters, my partners in crime, I love you, and I love the support you've given me. Your big sister will always be here for you.

Finally, to Angela and everyone at Tehom, thank you for your interest in my story and for all of your efforts in bringing it into the world. I adore your mission, and I can't wait to be a part of it! I feel like I've found my people.

About Tehom Center Publishing

Tehom Center Publishing is an imprint publishing feminist and queer authors, with a commitment to elevating BIPOC writers. Amplifying authors from the margins bent on writing toward justice is our calling and joy.

In addition to traditional, independent publishing at no cost to the author, Tehom Center Publishing also offers one-on-one and group coaching that empowers authors in book writing, book marketing, and book entrepreneurship through an intersectionally feminist lens.

Learn more at www.tehomcenter.org/tehom-center-publishing

Printed in the USA
CPSIA information can be obtained
at www.ICGtesting.com
LVHW010757270324
775472LV00008B/81

9 781960 326669